TRICKED

FAIRY TALE REFORM SCHOOL

TRICKED

JEN CALONITA

SCHOLASTIC INC.

ISBN 978-1-338-18758-8

12 11 10 9 8 7 6 5 4 3 2 17 18 19 20 21 22

Printed in the U.S.A. 40

First Scholastic printing, April 2017

Series design by Regina Flath
Cover image by Michael Heath/Shannon Associates

For Kellsie Marchbanks. Although we never had the chance to meet, you've inspired me in so many beautiful ways.

How do you out-trick a trickster?

Pegasus Postal Service

Flying Letters Since The Troll War!

FROM: Maxine Hockler (Great Oak Tree, Tailsmen Forest)

TO: Gillian Cobbler (2 Boot Way)

Hi, Gilly!

I'm sooo bored! My ogress friends have been thrown into Fairy Tale Reform School for typical ogre stuff, like storming castles and pretending to want to eat people. (We don't do that. I swear.) So I'm stuck hanging with Mother and Father. Alva and Rose gave us ogres a bad rap, so my parents want to show how friendly we can be by helping lost travelers get to Enchantasia (most scream and run) and offering beverages to weary knights (who try to spear us). It's exhausting. The only fun I have is staring at the jewels on the travelers. What I wouldn't give to swipe a tiny onyx necklace. They wouldn't even notice it was gone! That's wrong...right?

I don't know what to do with myself. I feel like I'm a spinning top that goes nowhere. Last night I was so upset that I told Mother: "I don't want to live in the forest and be an old ogress like you! I want adventure!" She got mad and sent me to bed with one supper instead of the usual three.

What's new with you? Does Jack of All Trades School still smell like leather? Is Anna still hanging out with those candy swipers? Maybe she should get an FTRS warning. I miss FTRS! The Pegasus flying lessons, the moving doorways that almost take your arm off, the Wand What You Want classes... I wish I could get thrown in again, but that's wrong too...right?

Have you spoken to Jax? I saw him when his royal carriage was taking him and some fancy schmancy friends to the Pied Piper Rock Concert in Haddingford. He heard Rumpelstiltskin was spotted at FTRS. That's got to be wrong...right? Miss you!

Your friend,

Maxine

CHAPTER 1

Shoes for Thought

"Who can tell me the five most popular types of shoe leather?"

Mr. Hide is standing on a step stool and pointing to an image of a leather boot on our magical blackboard. His green goblin fingernails tap the board lightly, and I feel my eyes begin to close. He taps louder.

"Surely someone knows." Mr. Hide sounds bored. I'm not sure he likes Shoe Leathers 101 either. "This is on our quiz tomorrow." Still no response.

I twirl my quill and stare at the students sitting near me in our tiny classroom that sits inside a massive pair of lace-up boots. Drawings of glass slippers and giant-sized slip-on shoes hang on the worn leather walls. The room has no windows and only one door, which never seals up and disappears like the ones at my old school.

"*Anyone?*" Mr. Hide tries again. A pixie in the back of the class sneezes. It's so quiet I can hear the sewing machines whirring in the Find Your Shoe Style! class next door.

I stare up at the ceiling, where the top of the boot shows a view of the blue sky. A Pegasus flies overhead. I imagine it's Macho, my favorite FTRS Pegasus, who spots me and swoops down to rescue me.

"I'm waiting!" Mr. Hide sings.

I stare at the image of the boot glowing on the magical chalkboard. The lace-up is a mirror image of my own beloved boots. Worn and faded, the boot looks like it has seen some action. It's not shiny like the boots Mr. Hide is always telling us to strive to make.

The boot on the blackboard fades away, and I see Fairy Tale Reform School. The shining turrets, gray stone facade, and climbing ivy covering the walls are a welcome mirage. I imagine the grounds beyond the school, which lead to the darkened Hollow Woods where no student dares to go. I can practically see students magic-carpet racing and flying Pegasi. A pirate ship sails into my mind, and I watch it drop anchor in the lake where mer-folk lounge on rocks. Blackbeard comes racing off the ship and—"Ow!"

I look down at my desk and see the small peppermint candy that just hit me in the back of the head. I quickly spin around and glare at the students behind me. The kids in the back row look like they've swallowed a gingerbread man whole. Smug Hansel, with his weasel-like smile and jet-black hair, is sucking on a lollipop. His mischievous sister, Gretel, is twirling her long, black braids, which are tied with pieces of licorice. Hansel and Gretel always look like they've had a fight with a chocolate fountain. Both have stains around their lips from too many sweets, and spots of chocolate, flour, and other bakery-related messes mark their simple peasant clothing. Gretel looks right at me as she tosses a second peppermint to her new partner in crime—my younger sister Anna.

"Gillian, how nice of you to speak up!" Mr. Hide says. "Can you tell the class the five types of popular leather?" Hansel and Gretel snicker.

Sticky buns. "Waxy, patent, metallic, oily, and suede," I say.

Mr. Hide beams; his green-hued skin and large ears

make him look devilish. "You will make a fine cobbler, Miss Cobbler." He pulls something out of his shoe box–shaped desk. "I believe Gillian deserves our Golden Slipper award this week." I cringe as he plunks the heavy gold shoe on my desk. The thing weighs more than ten schoolbags. Mr. Hide thinks his *prize* is something we strive for. Instead, it's become everyone's goal *not* to have to drag the thing home.

Hansel jumps up on his desk. "Three cheers for the hero of the hour: Gilly!" The class laughs, but Mr. Hide says nothing. Hansel and his sister are known throughout the village for plucking candy from sleeping babies and pilfering rolls from the bakery. Everyone is a bit scared of them. Except me.

Well, and Anna, who likes the pair for some crazy reason.

An off-key trumpet signals the end of our school day. Hansel and Gretel are the first ones out the door, dragging my sister along with them. She looks back at me for a second, her cheeks candy-apple red, then takes off. I shake my head and place the heavy Golden Slipper into my backpack. I'll have to drag it with me to work.

Out in the village, the air is cool and crisp, and Enchantasia is alive with shoppers. Teakettle houses whistle to announce the arrival of kids getting home from school, while large boots unlace to let homeowners pass through their doors. A tea shop made of teacups and saucers wobbles perilously as a large group enters, and a giant fish tank gurgles excitedly as mer-folk pop up among the reeds. I can hear hammering at Mother Goose's Nursery School, which is being rebuilt, and at the three little pigs' places. They've wisely chosen to construct their houses out of brick this time around. The village square and the market are packed with Pegasi bringing packages and shoppers on errands. I watch a porter with his arms full of bags trail a group of girls in Royal Academy uniforms.

Jax. If Royal Academy kids are in the village, maybe he's here too. We've traded Pegasus Posts a few times, but I haven't seen him since we left school. His last post said something about getting back into FTRS, but who are we kidding? We all got the same exit parchments. Once you've learned how to be "good" at FTRS, you can't reenroll. They only take kids on the path to becoming villains. We reformed types have to seek school elsewhere. I tried explaining that to Maxine in one of our posts, but she's determined to find a loophole.

I step out of the way as a group of students rush to

Gnome-olia Bakery. We collectively duck as a magic-carpet student driver comes dangerously close to clipping one of the pushcarts selling caramel cakes.

"Hey, Gilly! Want to go to Pinocchio's?" asks a girl from my Soles: Why We Need Them class as others run ahead to the large shop that looks like a marionette stand.

"Sorry. I have to work," I say. Not that I want to go to Pinocchio's Puppet Theatre or Red's Ready for Anything shop. Kids at lunch were talking about Red's new protection charm kit and the red capes she sells. Supposedly the capes keep the wearer safe from all harm. For the love of Grimm. A cape couldn't have stopped Alva, the wicked fairy who menaced this village and Fairy Tale Reform School for months.

The girl shrugs. "Have fun making shoes!"

Shoes. That's what I should be thinking about. Not my former school. But I can't help myself. My eyes look to the hills beyond statuesque Royal Manor (where our ruling princesses, Ella, Snow, and Rapunzel, live, along with Rose, when she isn't in princess detention) and search for the turrets of Fairy Tale Reform School. What are they doing right this minute? I have no clue. Headmistress Flora has never checked in with me. My favorite professor, Wolfington, has been MIA as well. Kayla sent a post about Rumpelstiltskin being spotted on the grounds, but nothing since. Has my roommate forgotten about me too?

"Give it back!" I hear a small voice cry. "That's mine!"

My ears perk up, my heart races, and I glance around the crowded square to see who is in trouble. That's when I spot the darkened alley between Geppetto's Pet Store and Thumbelina's Children's Warehouse. I see a boy trying to grab a bag that says "Sweets" back from laughing Hansel and Gretel. *Candy hoarders.*

Wait. Is Anna with them too? I run toward them.

Hansel swings the bag over the kid's head with a lazy flick of his wrist. "What's in here? Sticky buns? Cinnamon rolls?"

"No," I hear the kid say in a wobbly voice. "It's peppermints for my mum's birthday."

"Eww! Peppermints?" Gretel asks in a whiny voice that makes the fairy pets on our block howl. "Toss them," she instructs her brother.

Before I can reach him, Hansel flips the bag over and candy rains down on the kid. Hansel and Gretel stomp on every piece while Anna watches. The kid starts to cry.

"*Hey*, Candy Thugs!" I shout. "Leave the kid alone." I snatch the bag back from a startled Hansel. I'm taller than him by an inch, even if we are the same age. "Magical Scroll flash! If you want sweets, you *buy* them." I glance at Anna, who looks away. Wait 'til I get her alone.

Hansel rolls his eyes. "Because that's what you always did when you wanted something, Gilly? You paid for it?" My cheeks color and Gretel laughs.

"No, and that's how I wound up in FTRS," I remind him. Just the name of my old school makes Gretel shudder. Or she might be gagging. She is sucking on a piece of candy she just picked up off the ground. Gross. "Now pay this kid for the sweets you ruined." Hansel and Gretel just look at me. "You've got the dough. Everyone knows you knocked over that Sprinkles Tasty Cakes cart."

"You can't prove that was us," Gretel says worriedly.

"Let's see…" I scratch my chin. "They found candy wrappers on the ground next to the cart, and a pair of almost identically sized flour handprints on the money box. You also had Sprinkles Tasty Cakes for lunch today." Gretel pales and looks at Anna. "Now pay up, or I tell my buddy Pete at the Dwarf Police Squad."

Hansel sighs. "Pay her." Gretel produces a small bag of change from one of her chocolate-stained pockets. She tosses it to the boy.

The boy smiles at me. "Thanks. Hey, aren't you Gilly Cobbler?" I catch Anna rolling her eyes. "You're a hero!"

"*Was* a hero," I say quickly. "Now go on home before these guys start with you again."

The kid runs off.

"Happy, *hero*?" Gretel taunts.

I smile with satisfaction. "Very." Hansel and Gretel begin to skulk away, and I grab my sister by the back of her coat.

"Gilly!" Anna cries. Gretel turns briefly, then takes off. "Let me go! I've got to catch up with my friends!"

"*Friends?* That's what you call those guys?" I ask. "They're stealing candy from kids who are the same age as your brothers! They're trouble, Anna."

Anna shrugs out of my grasp. "They're *fun*." I laugh. "They are! Not everyone has had the exciting life you've had the last few months. Enchantasia Village is the same day after boring day." She glares at me. "I want excitement."

Anna was so sweet before I went away to FTRS. What happened to her?

"You are doing something exciting," I say as if reciting a speech I've given myself more than once. "With Father's business doing so well, we get to do a lot of things we never did before. Like have three meals a day and wear new clothes."

"Who cares about dresses if you have nowhere to wear them?" Anna scoffs.

True. "There's the Shoemakers' Ball," I say, but even the name sounds dull. I sigh. "Look, we're Cobblers. This is what we do—make shoes!"

"Well, maybe I don't want to be a Cobbler," she says, and I can't help but wonder if she means that in more ways than one. Before I can ask her, Anna takes off, dodging an apple cart and a large carriage shaped like a pumpkin. I let her go. I know better than to start with Anna when she's angry.

I watch the carriage turn down Boot Way. Only one class of people travels by pumpkin coach—royalty. My pace quickens as I strain to read the words written on the side of the coach: Rapunzel's Hair Care—For the Royal in All of Us!

Rapunzel? If she's here, then that could mean…

"Jax," I whisper to myself with a smile.

Then I sprint to the shop to see if my friend is waiting for me.

Chapter 2

Catch Me If You Can

Jax!"

I fly through the front door of the shop, sending a rack of finished shoe boxes tumbling like dominos. Shoe polish containers burst open as they fall on top of a stack of leather hides. A guard in a gold-and-royal-blue uniform aims his sword at my chin.

"State your purpose," the guard says gruffly while my father looks on in horror.

"At ease, gentlemen," I hear a woman say. "This is a friend, not a foe."

Rapunzel appears from behind Father's shoe counter and ducks to avoid hitting a rack of boots that are being stretched on a rod above her head. Her voice is velvety, like the pale-pink dress she's wearing. There is no poof to her skirt, no tulle on her gown, and no jewels are sewn into her bodice. Rapunzel is a princess who prefers understatement over frills. She's kind of normal, which I never thought I'd say about a princess. Instead of waiting for me to curtsy, she pulls me in for a hug.

"It's good to see you," she says. "It's been too long."

"Two months," I say, thinking of the last time I saw her—when Jax, Ollie, Maxine, and I were sent home from Fairy Tale Reform School after receiving our pardons. I put on my stained brown apron that says "Cobbler Shoes," pick up the broken polish containers, and toss them in the trash. Brown ink stains my hands, and I wipe them on my apron. The ink doesn't come off. Typical. "Actually, two months, three days, six hours, and two minutes." Father does a double take. "Not that I'm counting."

"Of course. Why would anyone count the days they've been out of FTRS?" Rapunzel says, and I detect the humor in her tone. It reminds me so much of Jax. All of Enchantasia now knows the two are siblings and that they worked together, with my friends' help, to save the kingdom from Alva. Order has been restored to the kingdom. We're no longer being terrorized by winged gargoyles (they're all locked up) or Alva (she's been turned to stone and is on display in the dungeons of FTRS). Life is back to normal. Simple, peaceful, boring normal.

Did I say boring? I meant...*boring*. Sigh.

"Rapunzel has generously offered to help me promote the shop." Father holds up scroll ads for Cobbler Shoes. His hands and nails are stained black from all the polishing he's done today, and he has black ink on his forehead. He looks tired but happy. He loves coming up with new shoe designs and now, thanks to the princesses, he's got his prize design back—the glass slipper. Sales for them have been through the roof, and business has never been better. When Jack of All Trades School said I needed an internship, Father jumped at the chance to have me. "The princess says even royals from other lands are asking about Cobbler glass slippers," he adds.

"I was just at a Royal High Council meeting with Haddingford and Captiva, and all the princesses asked if I had any connections to get a pair," Rapunzel tells me. "The wait list is almost two months long. I told your father that at this rate, he's going to need to expand the shop and hire more workers."

"Can you imagine?" Father asks, his eyes bright as he looks around his small shop, which is bursting at the seams with equipment, boots hanging from every bit of ceiling space and glass-slipper boxes piled high in the corners. "We could open Cobbler Squared, and you and your sister could run it!"

Run my own shoe store? I pale. Most village kids would be lucky to have their parents pass on a successful business, but when I think of shoe polish and leather hides, I don't get as excited as my brothers do. Suddenly, I can hear the shoe-shaped clock ticking on the wall, and I realize I haven't responded. "That would be very generous of you, Father."

The princess looks at me curiously.

"Rapunzel is also putting a shoe ad in the *Happily Ever After Scrolls* that will be published for the ball," Father adds as he gets back to work sewing up a large, white leather boot that must be for a troll.

"We have over a hundred royals coming in for the ball later this week," Rapunzel says proudly. "Princess Ella is working hard to foster better relations with foreign lands."

"Is Jax going?" I notice I'm playing with my strands of purple hair and stop myself. What am I doing?

"That's part of the reason why I stopped by today," Rapunzel says, and I perk up. "I had no idea you didn't already receive an invitation. The party is this Friday at 7:00 o'clock. I really hope your family will join us."

She hands me a velvet envelope, and I pull out the scented, pink invitation. I look at Father hopefully. He takes the invitation from me.

"That's so kind of you, Princess, but truly, you've done enough for the Cobblers already," he says. "We have no time to sew something this week with our workload."

"I have my gown from the last ball I went to," I remind him, trying not to sound hopeful. "Only the bottom of the skirt got singed by the wyvern." Rapunzel smirks.

"What would your sisters or brothers wear, or your mother and me?" Father asks. I think of my family's simple wardrobe. It's been updated, but we own nothing fancy enough for a ball. Mother's gown from the Fairy Tale Reform School affair was ruined after the school caught on fire. "Thank you, Princess, but we will have to decline."

My heart sinks.

"Next time then," Rapunzel says kindly, then turns to me. "Jax will be so disappointed. He's at the tailor's in the village getting fitted right now, if you want to stop by and say hello." I look at Father. My shift should have started fifteen minutes ago.

"Go see your friend," he says with a smile.

He doesn't have to tell me twice. I'm back out the door and running down the street, narrowly missing a caramel cake cart. The scent of caramel makes me think of Ollie, and I wonder where he is these days. My last two Pegasus Posts to him have been sent back. Is he still sailing with Blackbeard's friends? I wouldn't blame him for not heading home. That kid loves the pirate life. The pirate life and caramel cakes.

I swing around the corner of Boot Way again and see the tops of steaming teakettles and magic carpets flying. Pete, the Dwarf Squad Police Chief, passes by on a tall horse with Olaf, his henchmen, walking alongside him. The two of us nod. We've developed an understanding since I got out of FTRS. I don't bother him. He doesn't annoy me. I spin around the crowded square looking for Jax and spot a group of finely dressed kids in navy-and-gold uniforms. They're standing in front of Combing the Sea. I hear high-pitched laughter and see a tall boy with curly, dirty-blond hair is holding court.

"Jax!" I yell, unable to stop myself.

Jax's violet eyes light up when he sees me. "Gilly!" With a slight bow, he excuses himself from the fancy schmancies and runs over.

The two of us stop feet from each other.

I am the one who finally pulls him in for a hug, remembering too late I'm still wearing my apron and it's got shoe polish all over it. Crumb cake.

"Sorry!" I try to rub the polish off his RA gold sash.

"No biggie." Jax points to my head. "But you've got some on your forehead."

I try to rub the mark off but assume it's still there. Whatever. I see his friends watching, but I ignore them. Jax is my friend too. Actually, he was my friend *first*.

"Did you talk to Rapunzel?" he asks. "You've got to come to the party this week. All these neighboring royals are going to be there. The Little Mermaid borrowed a massive ship for the royal court to use for the party. They want the world to know Enchantasia is a safe place to visit and are hoping the party can do some damage control. They got Patacake BakersMan to make all the food!"

"I can't go," I say. There's no way I'm telling him my

family has nothing suitable to wear to a royal party. "We have plans Friday."

"Plans?" Jax looks disappointed. He adjusts one of the gold buttons on his double-breasted jacket. "What could be more important than attending Enchantasia's biggest ball?"

"Important things," I stutter, thinking fast. "Besides, if you really wanted us to go, you should have given us more notice. Madame Cleo says an invite should be handed out four weeks in advance."

"Unless an ogre invasion or a wicked fairy's hostile takeover causes invites to go out late," Jax teases. "Come on, thief! You have to come. We haven't talked in forever. You never returned my Pegasus Posts about getting resentenced to Fairy Tale Reform School. What do you think?"

At the mention of our former school, a mother walking with her baby holds the child closer and gives us the evil eye.

I shush him. "Most people aren't trying to get thrown back into reform school."

"Most people don't realize how cool that place is." Jax pushes his curls out of his eyes. "Royal Academy is the exact opposite. It requires you to attend all these royal workshops on topics like princely behavior and how to save a damsel in distress." He rolls his eyes. "I miss our fun, and I miss you. I'm sorry the invite was late. I would have told you sooner, but this is the first time I've been allowed to go to the village since we broke out and caused all that trouble."

I think of the day we toppled an apple cart, were chased through the village with Pete on our tails, and snuck back to FTRS in a Pegasus carriage. "Good times."

Jax raises an eyebrow. "Maybe not good, but definitely adventurous times." The two of us laugh.

"Have you heard from Ollie?" I ask.

"I heard he slipped onto Pete the Cheat's ship to avoid heading home," Jax says. "At least that's what a pirate visiting the manor told me. My posts keep coming back. I've heard from Maxine, but Kayla hasn't written at all."

"She's probably having too much fun with Jocelyn," I grumble.

Jax smirks. "You sound jealous."

"I'm not jealous!" I scoff. "It's not like I miss having a fairy roommate that used to work for a villain."

A fancy schmancy with a bright-pink bow walks over. She's pulling at her hair. "Hi, Jax."

Note to self: Never play with your hair again.

"We have to catch a Pegasus coach back to Royal Academy." She gives me the once-over, starting at my messy hair and moving to my stained apron and have-seen-better-days lace-up boots. "Are you done talking to this villager so we can get going?"

"*Villager?*" I snap. "I'll have you know I saved your pricey behind a few months back—and everyone else's in this village too."

The fancy schmancy's jaw drops, and I practically sneer at her.

"Thanks, Genevieve. I'll catch the next one," Jax tells her and steers me away. "Madame Cleo would be very disappointed. Where are your manners?"

"She started it!" I gripe. "Those fancy schmancies and royal wannabes…they're the ones who give royals a bad name! I was just—"

Kaboom!

A firework goes zooming past our heads, and Jax and I drop to the ground to avoid getting hit. It hits the village clock tower and explodes. The Humpty Dumpty statue on top of the clock topples to the ground and cracks. People scream and run for cover.

Zoom! Zip!

More fireworks fly past us, and people begin diving in all directions. A magic carpet goes skidding into a Rapunzel Hair Care cart and sends shampoo bottles flying. I can see the fireworks shooting out of the roof of Red's Ready for Anything like it's Royal Court Commemoration Day. Jax and I spring into action. I direct confused villagers away from the mayhem, while Jax rushes some peddler carts out of the way. A firework hits Pinocchio's Puppet Theatre, and one of the marionettes in the window is toast.

"How did this happen?" I ask a troll thundering by.

"Someone broke into Red's storage room and set off all the fireworks at once!" he says. "It blew the roof off! Red had to evacuate!"

"For the love of royals, who would do something that foolish?" Jax asks.

"Maybe someone who wanted to create a distraction so they could pilfer some area shops?" I guess. Jax looks at me. "What? I might have tried something like this once myself."

"*Clear the way! I have the criminals!*" Pete cries, and a crowd gathers to see who Pete is marching through town like a prize. "No need to panic, peasants! I have saved the day! These three are headed to FTRS!" People cheer.

"Wow, the third offense for all three? Brutal," Jax comments as we strain to see who the culprits are. I bet it's one of Patacake BakersMan's sons. Or Jack Be Nimble. He's been known to slip in and out of shops easily with lifted loot. I stand on my tippy-toes to see. I hear a gasp and realize it is my own.

"Anna?" I freak.

Hansel, Gretel, and my baby sister are in cuffs!

Their faces are covered in ash and soot from fireworks powder. Hansel and Gretel look thrilled, but Anna seems frightened. I break through the crowd with Jax behind me and stop in front of Pete's horse. "There must be some mistake! This is only her first offense!"

"Second!" Pete sneers at us. His horse neighs nervously at the sounds of the fireworks, but Pete grabs the reins tighter. "Her first was helping you and your little friends escape capture that day in the village." Anna won't look at me.

Oh right. "Well, it's only her second then. You have to let her go!"

Pete smiles sickly and lets a scroll unroll in front of us.

I recognize the FTRS proclamation. "You get sentenced on your second offense now. The little guy in charge changed the rules."

"What little guy in charge?" Jax asks.

I grab the bottom of the scroll and look at the signature. "*Rumpelstiltskin?*"

"Anna Cobbler," Pete says with satisfaction, "you've been sentenced to Fairy Tale Reform School!"

Happily Ever After Scrolls

Brought to you by FairyWeb—

Enchantasia's Number-One News Source!

Change Comes to Fairy Tale Reform School

by Coco Collette

After five years of running the school she founded, Headmistress Flora (the formerly wicked stepmother) is handing over the reins to a new leader: Rumpelstiltskin, *HEAS* has learned. While the news has come as a shock to some parents and students, Flora assures us the move has been under consideration for a while. "When Alva threatened our borders and children's safety, Mr. Stiltskin came to our school's aid, offering us both protection and guidance," Flora said in a statement through school spokesmirror Miri. "I believe he is the right person to head our school during these changing times, and I'm thankful he is interested in taking on a larger role at FTRS." The former headmistress will stay on in a new role.

Not much is known about Fairy Tale Reform School's mysterious new leader. Rumors have long lingered about

Rumpelstiltskin's shady business deals, but no proof has ever been offered about his involvement in the troll-goblin war or the disappearance of several prominent magical creature families. What we do know is that Mr. Stiltskin, as he has asked to be called, has already made changes to the FTRS admittance policy. "Students will now be sentenced on their second offense," Miri explains. "Mr. Stiltskin does not believe in letting a child's bad behavior go on too long. He wants them at FTRS as soon as possible."

Miri added that he will continue to modify this protocol and may even change it to first offenses! Pete, the leader of the Dwarf Police Squad, sees this as a good thing. "Too many hoodlums get away with all sorts of mischief," he says. "Just today I apprehended notorious troublemakers Hansel and Gretel Sweetums and Anna Cobbler. They could use the hefty dose of reality that Rumpel is giving out at FTRS."

Mr. Stiltskin has put the school under a protection charm that does not allow unscheduled visits to the school, so few have actually met him. Even his magical background is unknown. Some say he's a troll. Others a goblin. Miri insists all will be explained once Mr. Stiltskin conducts his own *HEAS* interview next week. A welcome party thrown by the new leader is also in the works. "Mr. Stiltskin wants everyone to see the groundbreaking changes he has in store," Miri says.

Let's hope our royal court receives an invite. It's no secret that the princesses are not big fans of the well-known trickster and were less than thrilled to hear Headmistress Flora was stepping down. "They are looking forward to having tea with Mr. Stiltskin to hear his vision for FTRS," says a palace source. As of press time, the princesses made repeated requests to set up a meeting with Mr. Stiltskin and had gotten no response.

CHAPTER 3

This Is Not the Thief You're Looking for

Never once did I imagine this happening to Anna instead of me.

"Look at this, Gilly! They offer cooking classes now. They didn't have those when you went here." Mother is reading a pamphlet called *FTRS: Making Magic the Right Way* as we fly in a fancy FTRS coach that is being used to usher parents to school to sign over their children. The wax seal on her pamphlet says "Now run by RS." I assume that's Rumpelstiltskin.

We fly through a cloud, and the landscape changes to country roads where trolls lumber along and ogres hang from trees looking for villagers to bother. In the distance, I can see the Hollow Woods, looking ominous even in the daylight.

"They even have macting classes now," Jax says excitedly.

"You know, in preschool, I was Knight Number 4 in a macting production of Sleeping Beauty's story."

Mother frowns. "The last time I took the children to a macting performance, one of the fairies in the play accidentally cursed an audience member. The man quacks when he coughs to this day."

I steal the flyer from Jax. The word *macting* is flashing colors like Madame Cleo's hair. Below it is a photo of her and Professor Harlow with a group of students. Professor Harlow looks less than thrilled.

"It was gracious of you to come with us this evening, Prince Jaxon," Mother says.

Jax's cheeks flush, and I snicker. "Please call me Jax. And you're most welcome, Mrs. Cobbler. Rapunzel knew it was important that I help you get Anna released. My sister and the royal court have the ball preparations covered."

"That's very kind of you, *Jax*," Mother says uncomfortably. "'And may I just say, we don't believe that rumor that Princess Rose tried to help Alva take over the kingdom. Such nonsense!" She fans herself with a brochure that says "Mr. Stiltskin has the right ingredients for your child's success!"

"Rose did make a, er, thorny error in judgment," Jax tells

her. "She'll be fine, but the princesses have ordered a long rest to help her regroup."

"But not a long nap, right?" I ask. Sometimes I crack myself up. Mother gives me the evil eye. "I don't mean any harm! Even if the princess did try to use me as bait."

"She was under duress," Mother says, defending Rose, and I snort. She grabs another brochure and her eyes widen. "What's a Magical Fairy Pets class? It says students are encouraged to care for an orphaned magical animal to learn responsibility. How wonderful!"

"Dear, stop acting so excited." Father wipes his brow. "No one *wants* to see their children end up at FTRS." He looks at me. "No offense."

"This is all my fault," I tell them. "Anna's been acting out at trade school, but with my internship, I just didn't have the time to police her every move."

"You are not your sister's keeper," Father assures me. "You have set an excellent example since you went to FTRS. Anna's just gotten in with some rotten apples."

"Hansel and Gretel are the worst." I clench my fist. "They'd be foolish enough to try to steal a lollipop from a baby dragon if they had the chance!"

"Sounds like someone I used to know," Jax says, and I growl at him.

The coach is suddenly engulfed in a golden mist. We stop short in midair, suspended by magic.

"Halt!" a voice thunders. "Fairy Tale Reform School is private property. Trespassers will be dealt with accordingly."

"That doesn't sound good," Mother says nervously.

"I'm sure it's standard procedure," Father assures her as he looks out the coach's windows. The castle is completely obscured from view in this gold mist. "Although I don't remember this last time—or there being a protection charm."

"Rumpelstiltskin did it on Flora's watch," Jax says. "I guess it's still up."

"Alva is a stone statue," I remind Jax. "Who is he trying to protect the school from?"

"Protect?" Jax is pensive. "Or keep out?"

We peek through the small hole in the front of the coach and see the driver hold up a gold card. There is a tinkling sound like bells. "You have been cleared," the voice from beyond says. "Enjoy your visit to Fairy Tale Reform School."

The coach lands outside the large castle doors with the famed stained glass windows. Each pane represents a reformed teacher—there are an apple, a glass slipper, a full moon, and a crescent. A skull has been added for Blackbeard the pirate and so has…a cooking whisk? The doors to the school open, and an ogre in a blue FTRS uniform comes charging at us like a battering ram.

"Gilly!" Maxine smacks me so hard that I fall into Jax and my parents. "Sorry!" She pulls me up with pudgy fingers that are three times the size of mine. "I got so excited when I heard Anna was here because I thought, that means Gilly must be coming too because she'd never leave Anna here alone," she babbles. "Hi, Mr. and Mrs. Cobbler! Remember me? Maxine Hockler!" She gives them a crooked grin, and saliva slides down the side of her mouth and onto her chin.

My parents look slightly alarmed, but they wave at Maxine as they look around my former school with a mix of shock and awe. Something about the foyer looks different to me too, but I can't put my finger on it. The elf cleaning crew is working the hall with self-mopping mops like they always do. Suddenly, a student whisks down the hall on a magic carpet. A massive gold mirror in the foyer begins to glow, and the glass turns a multitude of colors.

"Mr. and Mrs. Cobbler, hello!" the mirror says sweetly. "Miri, the school spokesmirror. If you would be so kind as to follow me into the enrollment office, we have some entrance forms you need to fill out for Anna."

"Forms are filled out *after* Anna interviews with Headmistress Flora," I pipe up.

"Gilly," Miri sniffs. "*Great* to see you again."

I wonder if the mirror can see me glaring at her.

"Why don't you talk to your friend, and we'll meet you inside," Mother suggests and hurries after Father.

"If you must know, Gilly, we don't have time for informational interviews anymore," the mirror tells me. "We've accepted forty new students this month alone, and Anna is our third apprehension this evening. Oh, hello, Jax! Lovely to see you."

Him she's happy to see!

"Hello, Miri," Jax says politely. "Did you say FTRS has had forty new students this month? How can there be that many kids on track to be villains in Enchantasia?"

"Maybe they just got restless like me." Maxine plays with a strand of dragon's eye jewels. "I saw a traveler wearing a pearl necklace, and I wanted it so bad." She smiles toothily. "When I didn't hear back from you two, I thought you were already here so I stole the necklace and got sent back. Smart, huh?" Jax and I shake our heads no.

"Pete and the Dwarf Police Squad have had their hands full now that the headmaster has changed the sentencing guidelines," Miri adds, glowing red.

"Don't you mean *headmistress*?" I ask lightly.

"Gilly, don't expect me to believe you don't know Flora is no longer in charge," Miri says in a prickly voice. "Headmaster Stiltskin is."

The magical intercom system crackles to life.

"Good morning! How to Slay a Dragon and Steal a Kingdom with Professor Harlow will be held in the North Hall this afternoon while visiting Professor Zalik teaches Genies in a Bottle: How to Exploit Wish-Making Opportunities in the observatory."

"Um, those don't sound like the assemblies we used to have," Jax says.

Maxine's smile fades, and her left eye begins to spin in its socket. "There are all these odd classes now, and we don't get outdoor recess or Pegasus privileges much anymore either. We are stuck indoors All. The. Time. You'd think he's trying to churn out villains."

"Maxine, don't be ridiculous!" Miri laughs nervously. "You know the headmaster is just trying to prepare students for the worst-case scenario. Right?"

Maxine sighs. "I forgot our new slogan—'FTRS: If you can't become a better person, become a better villain.'"

"*That's* the new school slogan?" I cry.

"An important announcement: Wanding 101 has been canceled due to a wand mishap that caused a monsoon to flood a classroom."

"Wait, is that Flora?" I ask. She's been reduced to morning announcements?

"Students should report to the Dark Magic: What Can You Learn From It? seminar instead. For those invited to Mr. Stiltskin's baking demonstration, please meet in the new lower-level kitchen at 1:00 p.m. The rest of you are instructed to go back to your dorms and practice spells. The headmaster hasn't seen much improvement. Therefore, all outdoor activities are canceled 'til further notice."

I think about Anna being cooped up alone in her dorm room all day learning how to make a candle ignite with a spell. She'll be miserable! "I can't believe Rumpelstilt—"

Maxine smacks her meaty hand over my mouth. "*Don't*

say his name. Three times and he'll be standing here. You can't cross him, Gilly. He's not like Flora."

"Gilly! Jax!" Kayla comes fluttering down the hallway at warp speed.

"Are you trying to get detention again, Kayla?" Miri asks.

I'm all ready to yell at Kayla for being out of touch when she yanks Jax and me in for a hug. "Go home," she whispers in both our ears. "While you still can."

"Kayla, what is going on?" Jax whispers back.

"Smile and laugh," Kayla says. "'He's watching. He's *always* watching." Her amber eyes are full of fear, but she starts to giggle. "I know! I look great, don't I? Well, it was good seeing you. Have a safe trip home."

"I'm not leaving without Anna," I tell Kayla.

"He's not going to let her go," Kayla says quietly. "Just go home. *Please.*"

Jax and I look at each other. Rumpelstiltskin stole her family and turned them into trees, and now he's here in the same castle with her. Why isn't Kayla trying to make a move against him? I'm so confused.

"We're not leaving," Jax insists.

A swirl of purple smoke surrounds us and makes us

cough uncontrollably. When the smoke clears, the Evil Queen's younger sister, Jocelyn, is standing before us in her signature black gown with sparkly moons and stars patterned on it. Her black hair hangs in her face, making her dark eyes impossible to see.

"Time to go home," Jocelyn says. She begins magically pushing Jax and me toward the doors. No matter how hard we fight, our bodies keep moving forward.

"I'm sorry!" Maxine cries. "Don't fight. It will just make things worse."

Jocelyn is still pushing me when I feel her slip something into one of my hands. The two of us make eye contact for a split second as I feel the cool glass slide beneath my fingertips. I don't look down to see what it is. Instead, I slip the glass up my sleeve. "Ex-students are not welcome here," Jocelyn says. "Go! And don't even think of trying to sneak around the grounds near the Hollow Woods. I'll report you."

The Hollow Woods? Hmm… She's trying to give us a clue of some sort.

"Gilly? Jax? Please report to the main office first," Miri says. "The headmaster would like to see you. *Now.*"

Maxine, Kayla, and Jocelyn have the same uneasy look

on their faces. Released from Jocelyn's spell, Jax and I walk past them. Jocelyn grabs me by my apron. Her voice is barely more than a whisper.

"Don't even eat a crumb if he offers you something," she says softly.

"Let's go." Miri's voice is serious. "Mr. Stiltskin will see you now."

Happily Ever After Scrolls

Brought to you by FairyWeb—

Enchantasia's Number-One News Source

Meet Fairy Tale Reform School's New Headmaster: Rumpelstiltskin!

by Coco Collette

Name: Rumpelstiltskin's famous moniker is so powerful that rumor has it that if you say it three times, he'll appear instantly. We didn't get to try it. Mr. Stiltskin, as he prefers to be called, was already waiting when we arrived for our interview, and he brought chocolate rhubarb muffins with him. "They're made with my secret ingredient," he said.

Occupation: Newly installed headmaster at Fairy Tale Reform School. "I made Flora an offer she couldn't refuse."

Hobbies: Mr. Stiltskin is an avid baker who makes nightly batches of his mouthwatering muffins in a magical kitchen. "I want to keep my students well fed." He teaches an after-school, invite-only bake class that he says has a wait list to get in.

Strengths: "I'm excellent at making deals." He also

prides himself on keeping Fairy Tale Reform School safe. "No one can get inside that school unless I want them there."

Weaknesses: "I don't accept rejection well," he admits. "In fact, I never accept it. When I want to make a deal, a deal happens."

Check back for more coverage on FTRS's new headmaster, Rumpelstiltskin!

CHAPTER 4

Things Are About to Get Tricky

The office is so dark it takes a moment for my eyes to adjust. I've been in Flora's office numerous times for sentencing and scolding, but this looks like a completely different space. Gone are the tapestries, rugs, paintings of her daughters (a.k.a. the wicked stepsisters), and cushy chairs and couches. In their place are burnished gold walls and a stark, shiny black desk. The fireplace mantel is decorated with gold awards shaped like cooking ladles, a giant hourglass with tiny gold crystals, and an ugly-looking troll doll. Suddenly, I hear a tinny, high voice.

"It's nice of you to finally grace us with your presence. I've been waiting."

I look left. I look right. I even glance at the coatrack full of small scarves and tiny coats. I still see no one but Jax and my parents, who are crammed into tiny chairs meant for kids Hans and Hamish's size. I feel a nudge. Jax glances ever so slightly to the fireplace and that weird-looking doll again. I give an involuntary gasp as the doll jumps down from the mantel and takes a seat in an extra-tall chair that rolls out from the corner of the room. That is no doll. It's Rumpelstiltskin.

He looks like a toddler with a beard. I start to smirk at the thought, then see the cold expression on his face. "Sit," he insists. Stiltskin motions to the chairs.

I can hardly fit in the small chair. Jax gives up and leans on the chair's armrests instead. Stiltskin's chair is three times the height of ours. He takes a seat behind his desk.

"At last, I finally get to meet the famous Gilly Cobbler and Jax Porter," Rumpelstiltskin says.

He's smiling, but I can't help feeling the gesture is for my parents. I know immediately I don't like him, but I can't put my finger on why. He's definitely the sharpest-looking troll—or is he a goblin?—I've ever seen. From his gleaming white teeth (I spot two gold ones too), manicured black beard, and short sideburns to his shiny gold button-down shirt and silver pants, he is very put together. I notice a white button on his shirt lapel that says "Live to Cook, Cook to Live" in glittery gold lettering and wonder what that's about. He catches me staring and pulls a chocolate croissant out of the desk drawer. He eats half in one bite.

"I've been waiting for this introduction for a while," Stiltskin says in between bites. "A long while."

"You've heard of our Gilly?" Mother asks proudly. "I had no idea anyone outside Enchantasia had heard of her heroism."

Rumpelstiltskin strokes his beard. "Her and her friends' efforts are something I've kept a close eye on from afar. Anyone able to take down such villainy should be commended. I can see why Flora pardoned her." He looks at Jax. "And you, Mr. Porter. I'm surprised to see you here instead of preparing for your ball. Royals don't normally dirty their hands with such messy affairs."

Jax visibly tenses. "In Enchantasia, we stand up for those who have been wronged, sir. That's why I'm here. To tell you that the royal court has asked that you release Anna Cobbler from Fairy Tale Reform School."

"The royal court has no jurisdiction here," Stiltskin says without hesitation.

I inhale sharply. That's not how the school worked before.

"I make all decisions now, as I keep telling Princess Ella," he adds. "Besides, I just spoke with Anna, and I believe she can learn a lot under my tutelage." He turns to my parents. "Flora's approach was too soft. She didn't know how to teach students to survive in today's villainous climate. Look at one of your fellow heroes,'" he says, using air quotes. "Maxine Hockler has already been thrown back in here for bad behavior. My approach is tougher and steadfast. Muffin?" He pulls a tray from behind his back. It's bursting with oversize muffins drizzled in chocolate.

"Thank you!" Mother grabs one for herself and one for Father before I can stop her. "We came straight from work so we didn't have time to eat dinner."

Father takes a bite right away. "Delicious!"

"Gilly?" Mother points to the tray. "Aren't you hungry?"

I'm starving, but I think about Jocelyn's warning. The muffins don't look suspicious. They are the perfect shade of golden brown, and the rich scent of melted chocolate is mouthwatering. I can practically taste the muffin, which is odd. Stiltskin pushes the tray closer, and I start to drool. I lift my hand to the tray.

Jax gently pushes it away. "Thank you, but Gilly and I

had something to eat at the Three Little Pigs before Anna was, um, detained. Right, Gilly?"

I nod but can't help feeling disappointed. The muffins look so good.

"I'm sorry you're so surprised by Anna's sentencing, but blowing up Red's Ready for Anything shop is a serious crime." Rumpelstiltskin offers the tray again. "Are you sure you both don't want to split one? My chocolate rhubarb muffins are famous. The folks at *Happily Ever After Scrolls* can't get enough of them."

"No thank you." I wish I sounded surer. "I'd rather talk about my sister. Do you have proof she was the one who blew up Red's? All I saw were fireworks."

Stiltskin laughs in a high-pitched voice. "While I commend your dedication to your sister, I think we both know she needs help." He jumps from the chair to the front of his desk and sits down on the edge. His voice grows serious. "Everyone in this room knows she's been acting up at home. Hanging with the wrong crowd. Skipping classes at Jack of All Trades School. You yourself have spoken to her about this on more than one occasion—just this afternoon, in fact, when she stole candy from a child."

I inhale sharply. "How do you know that?"

"I know *everything*," he says with a smirk. "This may only be her second offense, but I can tell Anna is on a path that she won't be able to come back from if something doesn't change immediately."

Mother grabs Father's hand worriedly.

"Anna is fine at home," I disagree. "What she needs is to stop hanging out with kids like Hansel and Gretel. They're the ones who probably talked her into what happened at Red's in the first place."

Rumpelstiltskin scratches his beard. "Interesting... Hansel and Gretel told me setting off fireworks at Red's was Anna's idea."

I jump up. "They're lying!" *They have to be lying. Right?*

Stiltskin leans forward. "But you're not actually sure, are you?"

I'm quiet.

"Yes. I see it now." He scratches his beard. "Flora had you pegged. I've read your file, and I can see why she felt you suffered from hero syndrome."

"Hero what?" I start to laugh. *There's a name for what I did?*

"Hero syndrome is when a person creates a bad situation so that they can be the one to fix it," Stiltskin says, and I stop laughing. "Flora found it interesting that you and your friends were always in the right place at the right time to fight evil. It made us both wonder: How do we know your lot didn't let evil into FTRS in the first place?"

I feel like I'm falling. *Flora wrote that about me? I thought she liked me.*

"But you two have been pardoned so I'm sure her diagnosis was wrong." Stiltskin smiles. "It's natural for you to want to save your sister, but you can't. She can only save herself, and she'll do that by being at FTRS." Mother and Father nod. "You can go home and concentrate on being a shoemaker's apprentice. You're both exactly where you're supposed to be."

"I think Mr. Stiltskin is right," Father says. I whip my head in his direction. He's polished off one muffin and is going for his second. "Anna has been difficult for months. She needs direction, and I think FTRS is the right place for her right now."

"She's been acting out more since you've been home," Mother adds. "Maybe she's better off here, taking classes with children just like her, the same way you did. Look at what it's done for you!"

"She's not me. I can get through to her," I counter. "She's only eleven."

Rumpelstiltskin hands Mother another muffin. She swallows it in one gulp. "The earlier we get access to delinquent children, the quicker we can change their behavior," he says.

"I disagree," I argue. "Headmistress Flora taught us that the willingness to be good comes from how strongly you're loved at home."

Rumpelstiltskin smirks. "If that's true, what's your sister's excuse?"

I don't like his tone. "Listen, Rump, maybe—"

He starts shouting so loudly that I fall back into my chair. "It's *Mr. Stiltskin*! Don't *ever* call me Rump!" he says wickedly, and I feel a shiver run down my spine. His face is red, and his voice is so deep I can't believe it's coming from his small body. "I've been patient with you and your ridiculous reasoning about your sister, but this is my school now, and if I say she's sentenced, she's sentenced. So watch your tone, or I won't even let you see her before you leave. Are we clear?"

I glance at my parents and wait for Father to stand up for

me, but he's just eating another muffin! They merely frown at me as if I said something inappropriate. Thankfully, Jax looks as horrified. The room feels warmer, and I'm suddenly sweating. "I'm sorry, Mr. *Stiltskin*," I say softly, and he sits back down.

"Good girl." Rumpelstiltskin wipes his brow with a handkerchief. "See how easy it was to listen?"

"It's settled then," Father says, licking chocolate off his fingers. "Anna stays here and learns how to… Wow. What do you put in these muffins, Mr. Stiltskin?"

Mr. Stiltskin smiles as he walks across his desk and reaches into a drawer. He pulls out a scroll and a pamphlet entitled *Magic and Mischief: Why They Shouldn't Mix*. "It's an old family recipe. I'll be sure to have Anna bake you some and send them since I did away with visitation day."

"May I ask why, sir?" Jax asks as I clench my fists.

"The former headmistress was lax," Stiltskin says. "Children got away with mischief, and the school was far too vulnerable—wicked fairies were breaking in and setting fire to buildings, not to mention threatening the lives of students and villagers. Now that I'm here, order will be restored. This is the safest place to be in Enchantasia."

"Makes sense," Father says, and then he signs away Anna without even reading the contract. Mother does the same. "Shall we go?"

Rumpelstiltskin smiles thinly. "I've packed you extra muffins for your journey home. And look for scroll updates from me about Anna's welfare. Miri!" he barks. "Please send Anna Cobbler in to say a *brief* good-bye."

Anna steps into the room wearing Fairy Tale Reform School's pale-blue uniform. Gone is the tough-girl attitude I've seen lately. Right now, she looks scared. When she sees Mother and Father, she bursts into tears. Mother hugs her.

"Oh now, child," Mr. Stiltskin says. "Don't be sad! You're going to fit in nicely here. Now say good-bye."

"Gilly?" Anna reaches for me uncertainly.

"I'm here!" I step forward, but Stiltskin blocks my path.

"We'll take good care of her." Rumpelstiltskin nudges my parents, Jax, and me to the door. "Anna? Let's go now, dear." He motions for my sister to move through a new doorway that appears in the office.

"Wait!" I cry, trying to get to her. I push Stiltskin, but he holds me back. Father grabs my hand and tries to pull me out the door to where Jax and Mother are waiting.

"Gilly, I—" Anna starts to say.

She's through the door before she can finish the sentence. My last image of my sister is her teary face as Stiltskin closes the door behind us, a look of satisfaction written on his face.

CHAPTER 5

Don't Be a Heel

Something isn't right.

It's been three days, and Mother and Father haven't mentioned Anna *once* since we left Stiltskin's office. My Pegasus Posts to Anna keep coming back—apparently he's halted those too—and I can't reach anyone at FTRS to find out what's going on with my sister. I've tried repeatedly to talk some sense into my parents, but they keep changing the subject and talking about their silly FTRS gift bags. Mother has been wearing an apron around the boot that says "Mr. Stiltskin has the Recipe for Success at FTRS!" while Father has been showing everyone his school handkerchief with the Fairy Tale Reform School crest printed on it. Han, Hamish, and Trixie ate the chocolate rhubarb muffins before I could stop them. Now everyone is walking around the boot saying things like, "Rumpelstiltskin is going to make Enchantasia great again."

For the love of Grimm, how can my family be so easily tricked?

I feel as mad as a hatter. I need to do something, so I send Jax a Pegasus Post asking him to meet up with me before the ball tonight. Now I'm sitting on a stack of magic carpets for sale at the local Arabian Nights shop. I can see him coming from a distance. He looks every bit the prince in a gold-and-royal-blue double-breasted jacket and gold pantaloons.

I jump up and grab his hand. "We have to break into Fairy Tale Reform School and steal Anna and our friends," I blurt out. "If we leave now, we can steal a few Pegasi and be flying over the Rootrum Mountains before bedtime." I pull on his arm. "Come on!"

"Whoa." Jax digs in his heels. "Let's think this through, thief. Stiltskin has the school under a protection charm. We can't break in, and even if we could, he'll know we're there and capture us before we even make it to the dorms—or send out people to hunt us down. This plan will end badly."

"It won't," I insist, but I know in my heart he's right. I

plop down on the magic carpets again. Jax sits next to me, and the top rug begins to lift off the ground.

I try to remember how to will the carpet back to the ground like we learned in Magic Carpet Racing Club. "Hey! Rug! You've got a prince on here, and you're going to make him late to his own ball!" The carpet doesn't listen.

"I don't think you're supposed to talk to it like that." Jax pets the rug like it's a dog. "Thanks for the ride, but we both have plans, so do you think you could descend?"

The carpet begins to lower ever so slightly, then shoots back up.

"Great. This rug belongs at Fairy Tale Reform School like the rest of us," I grumble. "Hope you like muffins!" I shout at the carpet.

The store owner must hear me because he runs out of the shop. "Don't worry, you're tethered. Blue will set you down when he's good and ready." I look down and see the rug is tied to a wheel on the ground far below.

"Great. Now I've made you late." I sigh. I thumb the rug's Oriental pattern of royal blues, greens, and gold.

"I'm sure no one will even know I'm missing," Jax says. "Besides, it's more important I stick with you and keep you from doing something foolish. You can't break back into FTRS."

"Yes I can," I say stubbornly.

"Can't," Jax insists.

"What am I going to do? Leave everyone we care about to turn rotten under Stiltskin's rule?" The rug bucks at the mention of Stiltskin. I give it a pat. *Good boy.*

"No, but we need an actual plan before we go charging to the rescue," Jax says. "I told you something was up at FTRS. Why didn't you write back when I wrote about Stiltskin being seen there?"

"I have a life outside of FTRS, you know," I say defensively. *So why are you so bored?* a little voice asks.

A teakettle whistle blows, and I know it's the end of the workday. A few blocks away, Father is probably closing up the shop. Below, the shopkeeper begins taking in the magic carpets stacked near us. The Pegasus valet stand is putting the animals in the stables. The only area that is still hopping is the seaport. Hundreds of fireflies are lighting the way up the ramp of the largest sailing ship I've ever seen. It makes Blackbeard's look miniature. I can hear the music from here, and I picture royals and guests dancing in lavish outfits. Jax is watching the party too, and suddenly I feel the need to come clean to my friend.

"The truth is, I didn't write you because I was trying to fit in at home," I say quietly. "But nothing was how I remembered it. Anna was already hanging with Hansel and Gretel. The rest of my family was busy with their own interests." I look at the ship. "I thought I could go back to my old life, but..." I trail off.

"You couldn't go back to the way things were before," Jax replies as if he's reading my thoughts. "And when you're being honest with yourself, you're not sure you'd even want to. Pretending nothing's different just makes you feel—"

"Trapped," we say at the same time and look at each other.

Is Jax bored with Royal Academy and life at Royal Manor?

Could he miss Fairy Tale Reform School too?

The carpet rises higher until the rope stops us.

"It doesn't matter what we think," I realize. "We can't go back to FTRS either. You heard Stiltskin. Flora obviously thought we were trouble. She said we had something called a hero complex."

"You can't believe a trickster like him," Jax reminds me. "We all know he stole that school from Flora. He'll say anything to make you feel bad about yourself. We helped save that school and everyone in it."

"But look who's running it now," I say with a sigh. "And we've got no way to stop him from out here."

"We'd need a bigger crew to pull off something like that," Jax agrees. "Ollie's at sea, and Kayla, Jocelyn, and Maxine are in FTRS. We can't do this alone." We stare in silence at the busy seaport. I can hear laughter, but the party feels so far away. Even the fireworks seem to have lost their luster. Anna is stuck in a Flora-less FTRS with Rumpelstiltskin, and I can't help her.

"Blue!" the shopkeeper calls up to us. "Come on down! It's time to go in."

If the rug understands, it's not listening.

"Come on, Blue!" the shopkeeper tries again. "My wife wants to watch the ball from the docks. I need to get home!"

I lean forward to ask the shopkeeper what we can do to help and feel something fall out of my apron pocket. I catch it just before it falls over the edge of the rug.

"What's that?" Jax asks as I hold it up to the dimming light.

"Jocelyn slipped it to me at school." I put it in my apron for safekeeping. Now that I can look at it, I realize it's a glass slipper heel. "I'm not sure what I'm supposed to do with it. It's not like a heel is going to be able to help us get into Fairy Tale Reform School."

Jax smirks. "Maybe we're supposed to throw it at Stiltskin's head."

We both laugh so hard that we practically fall off the carpet. Blue rolls up his edges to keep us from plunging several stories.

Jax puts his head in his hands. "Crumb cake, this is bad. We have no way to help our friends or your sister, and now we're stuck hovering above Enchantasia on a carpet that won't land."

"Maybe the heel will help us," I joke. I put my lips up to the heel and start to giggle madly. "Heel, think you can help us come up with a way to get back into FTRS without getting thrown out again? And while you're at it, can you find Ollie and have him help us? Thanks."

Suddenly, I feel the carpet start to rumble, then sway back and forth. We both stop laughing and hold on as the carpet tugs hard on the rope beneath us.

"*Blue*, don't even think about it!" the shopkeeper warns.

Blue gives another hard tug, then breaks free and takes

off like a firework toward the seaport. It's all Jax and I can do to hold on to the carpet's edges for dear life. I close my eyes as Blue dives left, then right, shooting through the nearly empty streets. When I open them, Blue is flying over rooftops and stables before we glide straight toward Dwarf Police Squad headquarters where I see Pete's horse tied up out front.

"Blue! What are you doing?" I ask the rug as it flies directly at the headquarters' front door.

"We're going to crash!" Jax shouts.

We close our eyes and prepare for impact, but it doesn't come. When I open my eyes again, I see Pete running outside. He looks up at the rug, and Blue dives for him. The three of us scream as the carpet grazes Pete's head and knocks off what appears to be a toupee. *Fiddlesticks. We're in trouble now.*

Instead of flying off, Blue circles Pete over and over, refusing to let him bend down and grab his toupee. Pete's horse gets so worked up that it breaks free of its reins and gallops down the street.

"Gilly Cobbler!" Pete holds up a fist as Blue flies away. "I'll get you for this! Stealing magic carpets! Taunting an officer! You too, Jax Porter! Royal or no royal! That's one demerit! One more and you're sentenced to Fairy Tale Reform School again!"

Jax and I look at each other in awe.

I think Blue is trying to help us get thrown back in!

Jax pets the rug. "Nice job, Blue! What's next?" The carpet rocks right, then left, narrowly missing laundry that is hanging across the alleyway we've turned down.

"I think Blue is headed for the ball!" Jax says. "Ready to crash a party?"

Oh boy. Jax will get in so much trouble for this. I can see the *Happily Ever After Scrolls* headline already. "Jax, you should jump off or land on a rooftop and get away. Your father and sister will turn you into a gingerbread man!"

Jax's hair whips around his face. "No way! We're in this together. The only way to help everyone is from the inside, and the only way in is to flunk out."

I grin. We're a team. A team that is about to cause mischief at a royal gathering where that fancy schmancy Jax was with the other day is probably partying.

This is goblin-tastic.

"Okay, if we're going to do this, we need some supplies," I say. "Blue, let's make a stop at Red's." The rug makes a sharp right turn, and a peddler dives out of the way, throwing an armful of maps into the air. A map hits me in the face as we whiz by. I pull it off my nose and look at it. *The Mystery of the Goose and the Golden Egg.* I stuff the map in my pocket. Stealing is another FTRS offense. I can't wait to tell Pete!

Blue comes in for a soft landing next to a pile of open boxes on Red's Ready for Anything rooftop. Anna and her friends must not have set everything off before they were caught, and her loss is our gain. Jax and I jump off the rug and grab smoke bombs, skunk-scented confetti blasters, noisemakers, and fart guns (which have been known to ward off angry trolls; they hate the smell). Then we hop back on the carpet and take off again, headed straight toward the ship.

It's actually quite pretty, I realize, as we barrel toward the royal vessel. The ship has massive blue-and-pink sails and is detailed with gold adornments and carvings. Tapestries with the royal court crest hang from the rafters, along with pink and gold streamers. Jax and I duck when we see the Dwarf Police Squad patrolling the docks, but the dwarfs don't think to look up, and we fly right past them.

"Come in as close as you can, Blue," Jax says. "And don't stop flying!"

The carpet rolls up the top right corner and seems to

high-five Jax as it listens to his command. We circle high overhead as the band Gnome-More plays on the deck.

"There's Rapunzel," says Jax, pointing out the princess, who is swaying to the music alongside Princess Snow and some goblin princesses. "Sorry, Sis." Jax drops a smoke bomb onto the deck, and it explodes in dark-gray smoke.

I'm next with a skunk-scented confetti bomb that rains down on the deck, making people cough and head for cover. Yes!

Next, Blue flies to the other end of the ship, and I see Princess Ella partying with a group of fairies on her shoulders. She looks lovely in her signature blue gown, and I feel almost bad about what we're going to do. I shoot the fart blaster into the air, and the sound makes everyone jump. That's when Jax drops another smoke bomb.

Blue takes off toward the crow's nest to survey the damage below. The beautiful party is going haywire. But haywire is not enough.

"Ready to do your worst?" I prepare a few more skunk confetti bombs.

"Definitely." Jax sets off a firework. "Blue, let's make mayhem!"

The party deck is crowded as Blue does a vertical drop, then pulls up just in time to swipe the tops of people's heads. We knock over fountains and swipe food off tables. People dive to the ground as Blue darts at goblins running in every direction. Rapunzel looks up just in time to see Jax pull a crown off a visiting prince's head and toss it overboard. I grab the cake off someone's plate as we whisk by, then look around for my next target. I smile when I see the rude fancy-schmancy from the other day.

"Blue, that way!" I say, pointing at the girl nearby. She catches sight of me seconds before I reach out and smush cake in her face. *Gingerbread, that feels good!*

"Gilly! Jax! No!" Rapunzel cries as Jax sends a cake hurling into the crowd, along with more fart gun blasts and skunk-confetti bombs. Next, we fly by the crow's nest again and set off fireworks.

People are running in all directions now. The Gnome-More musicians abandon their instruments and jump overboard. The Dwarf Police Squad has finally spotted us, but they can't catch us at this height, which is good because I can't decide: Have we been bad enough yet to be sentenced?

"We need a big finish," I say as Blue flies around the

ship again. "Something that really shows we belong in reform school."

Jax drops a soufflé in the lap of the King of Captiva. "Like what?"

Suddenly, I see the boat begin to sway. Rapunzel and Snow grab for the deck rails as the ship rocks like it is in the middle of a major storm. Blue flies out of the way of a rafter that sways dangerously close to us. We pull up just in time to see a pirate ship barrel toward the royal vessel at warp speed. Uh-oh.

"Abandon ship!" I cry in a panic to the guests still on board.

Rapunzel grabs Snow's and Ella's hands, and the three jump into the waters below. The remaining guests do the same as the pirate ship crunches into the vessel, breaking three rafters and sending the remaining flags into the sea. When the dust and the smoke clear, a short, dark-skinned boy wearing a bandanna and an eye patch jumps to the bow of his ship and looks around. When he sees us, he waves.

"Flapjacks, you guys are really here!" Ollie shouts. He's got dirt on his chin, his white shirt and vest are in tatters, and his pirate pants are torn up. He's definitely seen some action since we last saw him. "I got your distress call!" he says, and Jax and I look at each other in bewilderment.

The glass slipper heel!

"A pirate never lets a scallywag down," Ollie says, then thinks twice. "Well, he does, but I could never leave you guys. Life isn't the same without you." Blue descends so that we can jump off and stand with Ollie.

"Cuff them!" I hear Pete cry. "Those three are being sentenced to Fairy Tale Reform School!"

Sweeter words have never been said.

"On a first offense?" Ollie asks. "Sweet. I've missed that place."

"And we've missed you." I give him a hug.

The Dwarf Police Squad races up the ramp as the three of us keeping hugging one another, then hold our hands out for cuffs. Pete looks confused.

"Aye, this feels good," Ollie says as Pete clamps the metal over his wrists. "We're headed back to FTRS together!"

CHAPTER 6

Bad Apples

When Pete and Olaf throw Jax, Ollie, and me through the doors of Fairy Tale Reform School, our friends are waiting. A cheer rises up in the foyer, and then Kayla and Maxine hug us, while Jocelyn leans against a table and peels a bright-red apple with a paring knife. Poetic.

Pete pushes our friends away. "Miri!" he yells. "I've got three more for ya—repeat offenders."

Miri's foyer mirror begins to glow red. "Oh, I already heard. *Somehow* their friends knew they were coming." She clears her throat.

Maxine points to her large head. "Ogre intuition. It's very powerful."

Pete unlocks our handcuffs. "Yeah, well, tell Mr. Stiltskin not to let them out so easily this time."

"Oh, I don't think you need to worry about seeing this group for a while," Miri says ominously.

"Good." Pete narrows his beady eyes at me. "None of your parents are coming either. Second time in, they just get a scroll sent saying you're here. Your repeat stay in this joint is not going to be as peachy as the first."

"I wouldn't exactly call our first stay peachy," I mumble.

Ollie nods. "True! We were almost killed by a wicked fairy twice, and part of the school burned down."

Pete grins wickedly, revealing rotten teeth, then begins walking out. "This will be much worse. Enjoy your time with the trickster, thieves." Olaf and Pete slam the large doors to Fairy Tale Reform School shut. I can still hear them both laughing.

Miri sighs. "I'm not going to give you the big FTRS speech because you already know it, but make sure you go over your new school handbook." Three scrolls appear in our hands. "All the rules have changed. The headmaster has very specific ideas, and if you don't follow his orders, the punishments are much worse than detention with Madame Cleo. Am I clear?"

Miri almost sounds frightened. I push any fearful thoughts

out of my mind. "Yes. Now about dorming… I want to be with my sister Anna."

"She's rooming with Gretel. You're with Maxine," Miri says flatly as Maxine cheers. "Jax and Ollie, you're together." The two high-five. "Stop sounding happy! This is a reform school."

"I'm not happy," I complain. "No offense, Maxine, but I wanted to be with my sister." I keep seeing Anna's terrified face over and over again. I have to see if she's okay.

"Then you should have gotten thrown in the same night as her," Miri snaps. "Now, if you're all settled, I have four other children to process, and they're getting ready to go in and meet with Mr. Stiltskin."

"Ooh! Are we meeting with him too?" Ollie asks excitedly, and we all look at him. "What? I want to meet anyone who is supposedly shorter than me."

"The headmaster will not be briefing you," Miri sniffs. "He said he did not feel it was important to meet with children who weren't smart enough to retain their original lessons at the school."

Ouch. Okay, so maybe we should have considered Stiltskin's temper when we thought about doing this. How am I going to convince him to release Anna when I can't get near him?

"Run along now," Miri tells us. "You should remember the way."

Her mirror goes dark, and I watch the foyer behind us seal up. A new hallway appears where a portrait of the royal court was moments before. The new hall is empty except for an elf cleaning crew that is sweeping up straw. Where did that come from?

"It's been a long night," Jax says. "Why don't we all get some sleep and talk about things tomorrow? I'm sure Anna is sleeping anyway."

"She's Stiltskin's favorite," Maxine says brightly. "She's already in his invite-only baking club."

Jocelyn snorts. "She fits right in with that group." I look at her.

"No offense, Anna's just so different from you," Kayla says awkwardly, and my friends look anywhere but at me. I have a feeling that is not a compliment. Kayla quickly leans in for a hug. "Anyway, I can't believe you guys are here! I mean, I can because we gave you that shoe heel, but..." Jocelyn clears her throat. "I mean, see you in the morning!" She shakes her head at me as we all head to the dorms.

"What's your problem?" I snap.

"*You*, Cobbler," Jocelyn whispers heatedly. "I slipped you that heel so you could get far, far away from here and take your brainwashed sister with you! Not so you could wind up back here in this mess."

I'm not sure what to say. Then I hear meowing. A cat is coming down the hallway. The small black cat winds its way around Jocelyn's legs. It blinks its eyes at us.

"Cute kitty." Ollie bends down to scratch it.

"Don't!" Jocelyn barks, pulling his hand away right as the cat coughs up a fireball. We all jump out of the way. "Great! It must be after nine. I have to get Miss Matched in her crate." Jocelyn picks up the cat, then wraps her cloak around her and disappears in a cloud of smoke.

"Uh-oh, I better get Peaches to bed too," Maxine says worriedly, and her eye begins to spin at an alarming rate. "Come on, Gilly. We should get to our room. *Fast.* You'll love Peaches!"

"You won't," Kayla whispers. "Hide everything."

***

Kayla was right. Peaches is no peach.

"I'm sorry!" Maxine cries as I examine the large hole in the front of my brown dress the following morning. "She must have been hungry. I usually get her breakfast by now, but I didn't want to leave her, um, alone with you."

"*Quack!*" Peaches screeches in agreement.

The sound pierces my ears. She—or he—is the ugliest duck I have ever seen. Or maybe she's a swan. Aren't swans supposed to be ugly? Peaches is muddy brown with a green beak and a giant red growth hanging from her chin, with a large tuft of white hair on top of her small head. But her beady eyes make me the most uncomfortable. They're the color of sand. I feel like she can see right through me.

"*Quack!*" Peaches nips my finger.

"Ouch!" I pull away. I take off my store apron and place it on the bed. "Why do you have him anyway?"

"*Her.*" Maxine picks up the duck in her large hands and rubs its backside. "Peaches is supposed to be in a cage in our Magical Fairy Pet classroom at night, but I can't bear to leave her. The other animals bully her."

I eye Peaches skeptically. "Are you sure it's not the other way around?" Peaches hisses. "Wait. Does she understand me?"

"I don't know," Maxine admits. "All I know is Peaches

picked me. All the pets pick their owners and show them their magic when they feel comfortable in their surroundings." Maxine frowns. "Peaches is the only pet that hasn't done anything out of the ordinary yet. She just eats things she shouldn't and then sometimes… Uh-oh."

Peaches makes a strange sound as her neck rocks back and forth. Maxine holds the duck at arm's length as it throws up the remains of my Cobbler Shoes apron and the key to the store that was inside the front pocket. Maxine puts Peaches down, and she waddles away happily.

"I'll clean up this mess," Maxine says. She sprays Elf Refresh Spray on the throw-up, and it turns blue, then sparkles before disappearing with a *zap*. That stuff works wonders. I always wished we could afford it at home. Although I guess now we can.

I hold up what's left of my apron, then glance down at the extra-large nightgown Maxine lent me. "That's great, but what am I going to wear? My parents haven't sent my stuff yet."

Maxine brightens. "Not true! Your uniform already arrived. It's hanging in the closet."

I make my way to the closet, avoiding the duck. Sure

enough, the bright-blue jumper that I despised is in there. My striped tights and ugly black shoes are at the bottom of the closet as well. I'm not touching those. I'm keeping my brown lace-up boots that Father made me. I scoop the boots up and put them on the shelf above the clothes. I don't want Peaches getting her beak on them.

Maxine gives the floor one more wipe. "There! Now we can get breakfast." Peaches quacks again. "For you too, Peaches." Maxine's one eye begins to roll wildly as she looks at me. "So do you think you could try living with Peaches? I'm afraid Headmast—*Professor* Flora—will kick her out of the program if she acts out again, and I don't know where creatures who can't be fairy pets are even sent. Peaches already has two strikes against her for biting other animals."

The duck looks at me as if to say, *You heard the ogre. Keep your mouth shut.*

I'm not crossing Peaches. "She can stay." Maxine grins. It's the least I can do after turning my back on Maxine that time she wanted to be a… Wait a minute. I grab for a pink hanger in our closet and knock several down in the process.

"*Quack!*" Peaches comes running at the shiny, annoyingly cheery band of pink satin.

I hold the sashes out accusingly. "What are these doing here?"

"Isn't it great?" Maxine pulls one of the sashes from my hands. "We're back in the Royal Ladies-in-Waiting! They're getting a new school advisor."

A perfumed note is pinned to the sash.

We missed you! See you at your first meeting. Tessa

Crumb cake. They know I'm here. I thought I was free.

Maxine twirls around in her sash. "Gosh, it feels good to be back!"

A sister I'm not allowed to see, a headmaster with questionable intentions, and a duck that wants to kill me.

Good doesn't feel like the right way to put it.

CHAPTER 7

Change, Change, Change

I'm starving, but Maxine won't let us eat breakfast in the cafeteria. Apparently Professor Harlow demands we get all our food from her until she figures out what Stiltskin is putting in those muffins (and everything else the students eat).

The Evil Queen may be able to cook up a poison potion, but she cannot make a decent pancake. I toss the rock-hard disc into a trash can as we walk to our first class, which is Magical Fairy Pets. Maxine is trying to explain all the class changes since I've been at FTRS. It's hard to hear her when students are running down the halls and acting up. Where is Miri hiding?

"Headmistress Flora has been running the class for a few weeks," Maxine tells me, ignoring the chaos around us. "Stiltskin wanted to cut it, but Harlow convinced him to keep it. Something about every great former villain needing a creature sidekick—and Peaches picked me right away! She bit my thumb with her little beak and… *Ouch!*"

A running troll hits Maxine in the shoulder and keeps going.

"You could at least say sorry!" I shout.

The troll turns around. I jump when I notice he only has one eye. He marches over and knocks all my books out of my hands.

"*You* watch it," he growls.

I smile, fold my arms, and wait for this newcomer to FTRS to learn his lesson. Any second now Miri's mirror will start to glow, and she'll be barking at this kid about detention with Madame Cleo.

Any second now…

The troll catches me staring at the mirror and bursts out laughing.

"You waiting for Miri?" he asks as kids continue to run by. "She won't mess with me. I'm with *him*." The troll flashes me a gold RS badge on his uniform lapel. Before I can ask what it's for, he turns and knocks books out of the hands of two goblin girls walking by.

"Why, that overgrown rock…" I mumble, watching him

retreat. I notice a wad of something gold hanging out of his back pocket and squint to get a closer look. Is that yarn? And in his other back pocket is a small gold book with the initials RS on it. I head after him.

"Don't mess with him," Maxine begs. I can still hear his loud laughter when he jumps into an open doorway. "Anyone that messes with Mr. Stiltskin's bake crew is toast."

"For the love of Grimm, Maxine," I hear Jocelyn say. She appears in a cloud of smoke along with Jax, Ollie, and Kayla. "You're knocking Harlow's toast again? My sister is keeping you fed. Who cares if her bread is a little crispy?"

"It was more than crispy," says Ollie, attempting to bite into a very burned bagel. He gives up and tosses it in the trash. "I think I'll skip breakfast today."

Jocelyn rolls her eyes. "I should have let you eat a muffin and join his Stiltskin Squad."

"Stiltskin Squad?" Jax, Ollie, and I repeat.

"Rumpelstiltskin's favorites," Maxine explains. "Like that guy who just knocked your books down. You can tell they're in the club by the special RS badges they wear on their uniforms. Squad members get to be in Stiltskin's baking club."

I snort. "Who would want to bake with him?"

"Anyone with half a brain," Jocelyn says. "Teacher's—or should I say headmaster's—pets who are in his baking club get later curfews and special privileges."

"The only way into his club is to fawn over him. Those who refuse to do that get punished for it." Kayla hands me her mini magical scroll. It has the FTRS schedule for the day on it. The words on the scroll flash bright red. Jax and Ollie read over my shoulder.

> *Kayla—Mr. Stiltskin feels it was inappropriate of you to skip his assembly, Why Rumpelstiltskin Is the Best Headmaster Ever! As punishment, all your extracurriculars have been canceled. Do not attempt to go to Wanding for Pleasure, Pegasus flying lessons, or the lecture you signed up for called Fairy Good: Learning What Magic We Can Steal from Our Flying Friends.—Miri*

"So basically you either eat a muffin and think he's a rock star, or you're banished to the dungeons?" Jax watches two pixies with RS badges spray-paint a mustache on a picture of former Headmistress Flora.

Maxine nods. "Pretty much."

The wheels in my brain start turning. "One of us has to get in that group and spy on them. We can find out what devious thing he's up to and get him kicked out—after he reverses the spell on Kayla's family, reinstates Flora, and gets Anna pardoned of course. I bet it won't take us more than a week or two tops."

Jocelyn creates tiny sparks with her fingers. "Save your breath, Cobbler. I've already tried. We all have. He wants no part of us—especially Kayla."

"I've tried to get in to talk to him about my family since the day he got here," Kayla says, and I have a feeling she might cry. "You know when my scheduled meeting is? Seven months from now! Meanwhile, the RS crew is in his office all day long."

"Great. He's onto us already," Ollie whispers. A group of fairies fly by carrying a basket of Stiltskin's chocolate-rhubarb muffins to class.

"Let's recruit someone else to spy on him for us," I suggest. "Like Anna."

Jocelyn starts to laugh wickedly. "You fool. Don't you see? Look around you. Kids *like* him. *Anna* likes him. They want to be on his good side so they can get perks. They're not looking for a hero to save them."

"But..." I don't understand. "Isn't the point of coming to FTRS to become *reformed*?"

Jocelyn shrugs. "Kids don't care about that. They'll take any chance they get to be bad. It's what they know. And if you take that from them, they'll despise you for it." A rotten apple comes whizzing past my head and hits Jocelyn in her shoulder.

"What are you whispering about, witch?" Hansel shouts. He and Gretel are walking toward us. I spot their RS badges right away. "End it now, or I'll have to report the lot of you."

"You're in his little club too?" I start to laugh. "Pretty pathetic inner circle."

"I'll say." Jocelyn stands beside me.

"Quiet, witch," Gretel sneers.

"Stop calling her a witch, *witch*," I say. "What's the matter? Crankier without any candy to steal?" Hansel makes a move toward me.

"Back off, Hansel," someone says.

And that someone isn't Gretel.

The small girl pushes her way through Hansel and Gretel and stares at me.

"Anna!" I rush over and squeeze her. She feels limp. "I wanted to come see you last night, but they wouldn't let me. Are you okay?" I look her over. She's wearing the same uniform as me, and her long, dark hair is pulled back with a black-and-white-striped ribbon. She smells like her Rapunzel shampoo, which means Mother must have sent our things.

Anna looks upset. Does she blame me for getting her sent here?

"Are you sleeping okay?" I ask. "Eating? Maybe if we ask him together, he'll let you move into my room with Maxine. It's big enough for the three of us."

"I'm already rooming with Gretel," Anna says flatly. "What are you doing here anyway?"

Hansel unwraps a piece of gum and gives it to Gretel. "Anna, we have to police the hallways. Come on."

"Just give me a second, okay?" Anna tells them. "I need to talk to my sister."

The two walk a few feet away and practice blowing bubbles.

"Now, tell me how you got thrown back in here—and why you did it." She looks skeptical. Smart girl.

I came here for you, I want to say. "Jax and I crashed the royal ball." I lean in close and whisper in her ear. "But don't worry. You're safe now. I'm here, and I'm going to get you out."

I watch her face go from disappointed to ogre-sized angry. "I don't need you to rescue me. I'm fine! You just couldn't stand that I was in FTRS without you, could you?"

My jaw drops. I thought she'd be happy I was going to bust her out of here. "Anna, I…"

She steps away. "You need to get to class before the bell. All of you. Go."

I start to laugh. "You're giving me orders now?"

"Yep." Anna points to her uniform collar. My face drops when I see the gold RS stitched onto it. "I can take care of myself just fine."

What has gotten into her? I grab her hand. "Anna, this isn't a game. He's dangerous. You have to stay away from him."

"You're the one who should stay away," Anna says quietly. "Stay out of trouble, Gilly. He's not a big fan of yours." Her expression is hard to read. "And at the moment, neither am I." She heads off with Hansel and Gretel.

I just stand there dumbfounded. What is going on here?

Ollie walks up next to me and shakes his head. "Looks like someone ate a muffin."

Chapter 8

Fairy Yours

I don't have time to figure out what's up with Anna because seconds later I hear a *pop!* and an arched wooden door appears in front of us. There are deep scratches and bite marks in the door and a broken gold nameplate below the small stained glass window that says "Magical Fairy Pets with Professor Flora."

"Don't worry about Anna," Maxine tells me. "I bet she just didn't have breakfast yet." She pushes open the door, and I hear an elephant. "Let's go in! This class will take your mind off everything."

Jax and I cautiously step over the threshold. It sounds like we've entered Enchantasia Zoo. There is a chorus of neighs, baas, squeaks, tweets, and other animal sounds. Ollie steps in after us, and a bird poops on his shoulder.

"Ollie, don't disturb Porter's falcon," says Flora. "He's agitated already, and I have a class to run." The former Wicked Stepmother looks exactly as I remembered her—salt-and-pepper gray hair, piercing eyes, and her signature long, bland green petticoat dress. With a wave of a wand—something I've never seen her use before—the mess on Ollie's shoulder disappears. "Take a seat in the front row," Flora says. She doesn't ask us what we're doing back here or say that it's nice to see us. "And don't wave your hands around too much in front of the cages. Sasha doesn't like sudden movements." We hear a loud roar.

"I hope Sasha's not looking for an owner," Jax whispers.

"Me too." I sit in the front row and turn my body sideways to look around. Anna isn't in here. Neither is anyone with an RS badge, which may explain why things feel more relaxed. Kids are talking near cages filled with animals. Some kids' birds fly haphazardly around the room, poking their beaks at the closed windows, while the mermaids' pets are already inside their tanks. One girl holds a sea horse, and I see another trying to swim away from an anglerfish.

Maxine waits 'til no one is watching, then lets Peaches walk out of her oversize backpack. Jocelyn's cat, Miss

Matched, sees the duck and hisses. There are shelves full of books and jars labeled "Food" that have various critters in them and containers labeled things like "Only for Unicorns," "Lion Sleeping Pills," and "In Case of Class Emergency." A lesson plan is written in tight, neat script on the magical chalkboard.

1. *Bond with your fairy pet! The more you get to know each other, the more it will learn to listen to your commands.**

   **Please exercise caution. If your fairy pet roars, hisses, bares its teeth, or shoots magic, see Professor Flora immediately.*

2. *Feed your fairy pet appropriately and at least three times a day, remembering to give it plenty of water.**

   **Remember that what goes in must come out. . .and you are responsible for your pet's cleanup.*

3. Help your fairy pet reveal its magical skills through training. The book *Fairy Yours: Unlocking Your Magical Pet's Talents* is quite helpful!*

   *If you find your pet trying to mind control you, please seek help ASAP.

4. Fairy pets should not spend the night in your dorm room! They must be returned before bedtime.*

   *Fairy pets are still animals. FTRS cannot be held responsible for any mauling, maiming, or other injury that occurs as a result of rule breaking. Stay safe. Put your pet in its cage.

5. Fairy pets are not meant to be used to break school rules or to steal, break, borrow, or destroy another student or teacher's property.*

*Don't let them convince you to do these things either. (See footnote under Rule 3.)

6. Fairy pets are not your slaves. They are your companions.*

*If you find yourself questioning whether you have become your pet's slave, FTRS offers deprogramming services!

I glance at Flora sadly. I can't believe she's been reduced to teaching this class. I feel like I should say something to her. I walk over to her desk, where she's sorting papers.

"Headmistress...I mean, Professor," I say awkwardly, but Flora doesn't look up. "I just wanted to say that FTRS doesn't feel the same without you in charge."

Flora looks up. "Then maybe you shouldn't have gotten yourself resentenced."

Fiddlesticks. She's not happy. I get it. I lean forward so that I can be heard over the elephant in the room. "I am here to help you. Maybe we could get rid of You-Know-Who together." I nod knowingly, and Flora frowns.

"Whatever gave you the idea that I needed a child's help?" Flora says coolly, and my jaw drops. "Especially a child who is so poor at undergoing a transformation that she can't stay good for more than a month? If I needed a hero to save me, Miss Cobbler, you would not be the one I would call. Take a seat, please."

My cheeks are burning as I walk back to my chair. I'm mortified. Stiltskin was right. Flora thought I had a hero complex! I guess I was wrong to think we got along.

"Everyone, please take your pets to your desks and we will begin," Flora says.

People shuffle to their seats holding large cats, a guinea pig, a real pig, and an ostrich, along with a baby elephant and a wolf cub that is licking his lips as he stares at the rabbit on the desk in front of him.

"I hope everyone has had a successful week caring for their fairy pets," Flora begins. "I've long believed this program should be part of the curriculum at FTRS, and I'm pleased Mr. Stiltskin agrees with me."

"You mean he hasn't taken it away from you yet," says a girl in the back row, and we all turn around.

The girl is taller than most of the students in here, and she has pale-yellow eyes and almost-white hair and skin. She mists her face with a spray bottle even though it's not hot in here. Weird.

"Miss Hayley Holliway, let's keep comments about our headmaster to yourself," Flora says stiffly, and I see her glance my way.

"Why?" Hayley asks, clearly enjoying herself. "Does it up my chances of not being asked to be in the Stiltskin Squad?" A few people laugh.

I like this girl.

"Miss Holliway, another outburst and you'll receive detention," Flora says. "We have much to cover today. I'd like to hear how you've been bonding with your pets and—"

"Mine bit a cafeteria aide," says a girl holding a raven. "How do I feed Horus?"

A goblin raises his shaky hand. "I'm afraid to take Sasha out of her cage because she looks like she wants to eat me," he says as he stands next to a cage with a small tiger.

"Mine peed all over Professor Harlow's office. She was *not* happy."

"Miffy eats my lunch *and* hers! Every day!"

"Professor Flora?" Maxine waves her hand wildly. "The other pets aren't being nice to Peaches so I think she'd be better off staying in Gilly's and my room."

"Let her!" agrees a sprite. The pet cage she's holding is so tiny that I can't even see what she has in there. "That duck ate three water bowls, a lamp, and a cabinet of magical pet treats this morning! If she stays in this class, she'll eat every pet in here—and maybe me." Peaches burps, and Maxine clutches her tightly.

Flora looks at the ceiling. "And I thought the royal court was hard to deal with," I could swear I hear her say.

A door to the classroom appears out of nowhere. It flies open, startling the birds, which quickly take flight. One escapes out the door.

"Mother!" Azalea rushes into the room in a bright-yellow ball gown, her hair half in curlers. "Dahlia won't let me use her fairy hair wand, and mine keeps glitching after only three curls of my hair!" She doesn't let Flora interrupt. "How am I supposed to finish my hair and put on my tiara for Rapunzel's arrival?"

Flora sighs. "Class, I will be back in ten minutes. While I'm gone, Gilly, Jax, and Ollie, please let a *pet* pick you as an owner. If you're smart, you'll tell them a little something about yourself so you get a good match."

"Me first!" Ollie jumps in front of the cages. "'I'm a pirate who is always up for an adventure. Any takers?" A cage on the top shelf begins to glow, and the bars disappear. A green parrot swoops down and lands on Ollie's shoulder.

"*Squawk! Mine!*" the parrot announces, and the class cheers.

Wow, that was easy.

"Jolly good!" Ollie feeds the parrot a treat from a jar on his desk. "Every pirate needs a parrot. How do you like the name Pete after my pirate captain, Pete the Cheat?"

"*Squawk! Pete! Pete! Pete!*" says the parrot.

"I'll get this over with next," says Jax, standing up. "Hi. I'm Jax or Jaxon, and I'm a member of the royal family who has—" A cage on the middle shelf begins to shake and bounce, and then the bars disappear. A small Chihuahua barks like mad, then jumps into Jax's hands. It's a small, white dog with a blingy, gold collar. It stands on its hind legs and begins to pirouette. "He's like a circus dog!"

Ollie got a parrot, the perfect pirate companion. Jax got an adorable dog. Maybe this pet-matching thing is for real. I step forward.

"I'm Gilly." I eye a cute, fluffy white kitten in a cage. "Let's see. What can I tell you about me?" I try to rack my brain for something brilliant. "I'm really friendly."

Ollie snorts. "You mean you're really bossy."

"And you are allergic to anything pink and girly," Kayla adds. "Even if you have a purple streak in your hair."

Miss Matched purrs in Jocelyn's lap.

"Don't forget to mention your hero issues," Jocelyn says.

"Stop telling them bad stuff about me," I snap. "That's my job."

"I thought your job was making shoes," Jocelyn says.

I glare at her. "My father makes shoes. Not me."

I hear a faint bell, but none of the cages are glowing, no bars are evaporating, and no pets are appearing. Where is my pet?

I hear a shriek. Some girls jump up on their chairs while a boy climbs a bookcase. Then I spot a small, brown mouse running across the floor. It stops and sits on my shoe.

"I got a mouse?" I cry. Jocelyn laughs. "I want a do-over!"

The mouse squeaks madly. Maybe it's unhappy it got me as well.

"Once you're paired, you're paired," Hayley says. She

scoops up the mouse, and the other kids move away as she holds the critter out to me. "Now you two should bond."

"You want me to bond with a mouse?" I say slowly. I've always been squeamish about rodents. They hang out in alleys and in garbage pails. They're not pets.

"Yes." Hayley pets the mouse's back. He (or she?) seems to like it. She holds him out to me again, and I hesitantly let the mouse crawl into the palm of my hand.

"He's cute!" Maxine says encouragingly. Peaches sniffs him, then turns her beak away. Even Peaches doesn't want any part of him. "What will you name him?"

"No clue." The mouse feels strange sitting in my hand. He's got a tail and beady eyes and…he's a mouse! "I think that's enough bonding." I quickly put him down on the table, and he squeaks again. Hayley picks him up and feeds him a small treat.

"Mice are sweet," Hayley says. "We had a lot of them around where I grew up." She takes a bottle out of her pocket and mists her face with water.

"Where was that?" Jax asks.

Hayley momentarily looks panicked. "By Gardener's Lake. My parents are fisherman so we spent a lot of time swimming near the docks. I mean, *on* them."

"That's where my family was from!" Kayla says excitedly. "Have you been to Fairy Hollow? Do you know a fairy named Angelina? That's my mom!"

Hayley seems uncomfortable. "No, Fairy Hollow was hard to get to."

Kayla looks puzzled. "It was right by the lake."

Hayley shakes her head. "Right! Maybe. I can't remember. Sorry. I'm exhausted. My unicorn likes to be fed at 5:00 a.m." She motions to a large window. Outside, I see a corral with a unicorn and a few horses.

"You got a unicorn? Why'd I get a lousy mouse?" My mouse scurries over to my hand and nips me. "Oww! You little garbage dweller!" The mouse squeaks angrily.

"Mice don't actually love garbage—that's rats," Hayley says. "Your little guy will love tight spaces. A boot. Some table scraps. He'll even sleep on your pillow."

"Absolutely not," I say. The mouse starts to squeak again.

"What a temper!" Hayley says with a chuckle.

"Me?" I ask.

Hayley looks surprised. "No, your mouse."

"So what are you in for, Hayley?" Kayla asks.

Hayley shrugs. Some kids don't like to reveal what they've done to get thrown in. "Nothing worth sentencing. I didn't know it was a crime to watch him on the docks."

Rumpelstiltskin. We crowd around Hayley who mists herself over and over.

"What did you see?" I ask breathlessly.

"Nothing!" Hayley starts to get upset. "He had a bunch of kids from school loading boxes on and off a boat, and I was watching. All his shipments have been coming out of the Gardener's Lake docks since he started here. When he saw me, he threw a fit and had the Dwarf Police Squad take me away. I didn't even get to say good-bye to my family."

A tear trickles down her cheek, then evaporates into thin air. Odd.

"What was in the boxes?" Jocelyn asks. "Did you see inside one?"

Hayley looks away. "Look, I don't want any trouble. I am going to do my time and get back to my family before they have to leave. If they do, I'll never find them."

She isn't making sense. She must be nervous. "You can trust us," I tell her. The annoying mouse squeaks at Hayley in agreement. I think. "What did you see? Please."

Hayley spritzes herself again. "I didn't understand why he was so mad. All he had in the box was hay."

Maxine giggles. "Boxes of hay? How much can our Pegasi eat?"

Jocelyn nudges her. "You fool. He doesn't care about the Pegasi!"

"Then what does he need hay for?" Maxine asks.

Kayla's face is grim. "He uses it for spinning hay into gold."

"I saw one of the Stiltskin Squad members carrying a wad of gold thread in his back pocket," I tell Jax. "Do you think they're helping him spin it?"

"Maybe," Jax guesses. "I thought the royal court confiscated all his spinning wheels when he moved into the kingdom again. He must have hidden some."

"Why does he need more gold?" Ollie asks. "He already controls the school."

"I don't know," I say. "But we are going to have to find out."

CHAPTER 9

Sisters in Arms

"Pitiful. Just pitiful."

Professor Harlow—who some still like to call the Evil Queen—paces back and forth in front of our fencing team looking particularly menacing in a black-and-dark-blue fencing suit with a paisley silk cape. "We have our first fencing meet against Shining Timbers Academy next week, and most of you can barely master a good jab, let alone win a duel. I don't even want to be associated with this group!"

"Does that mean you're going to let Blackbeard take over the club?" I ask hopefully. This is the first time I've seen Harlow since I've been back. She clearly hasn't missed me.

"Miss Cobbler, if I had my way, you wouldn't even have been allowed to try out for the team—repeat FTRS offenders should not be rewarded, in my opinion—but *he* wanted me to keep an eye on you." Harlow rolls her eyes. "Watch yourself, or you may find your next dueling partner is me, and I won't go easy on you." She whips her cape around herself and whirls away.

"For fairy's sake, do you have to tick my sister off every time you see her?" Jocelyn asks. "She was so mad she had to let you on the team that she burned dinner last night."

"What else is new?" I turn to face one of the fencing dummies. "Guess I better practice if I have to face Her Evilness next." I jab the dummy in the shoulder.

Joining the fencing team was something I didn't get to do the first time around at FTRS, so I'm excited to try it—even if Stiltskin is keeping an eye on me. I may not know how to beat him or how to get through to Anna, but fencing is something I know I'm good at. It's time to get to work. What to do first...

The dungeon where we practice is brimming with target dummies wearing fencing gear, and swords of varying lengths line the walls. Some might find the dimly lit room intimidating, but I think it sets the stage for an epic battle. I pull down my helmet and imagine facing an opponent. Suddenly, I feel my sword get knocked out of my hand. A second slash hits me in the arm, and I wince. Even though our swords are bewitched so they can't cut, they still hurt.

"Ouch, Jocelyn!" I hold my throbbing shoulder.

"Don't get your purple hair in a knot. I didn't challenge you to a duel," she says. She points her sword to two people in fencing gear standing behind us. "They did."

I look behind me. Their masks are pulled down, and their swords are ready for attack. I wait for Harlow to stop the madness, but she watches us with interest. The other girls in the club gather around to see what will happen.

"If it's a duel they want, I'll give them one," I say. Holding my hurt arm, I rise to one knee and grab my sword. I hear the figures laughing through their masks as they draw near, so I swipe low and hit them both in the shins. The sneak attack sends them to the ground.

"Nice one, Cobbler!" Jocelyn says.

I grab my sword and cockily swing it in the air before walking over to my downed opponents to remove their masks. I grab the shorter one's mask first, but before I can pull it off her face, the kid jumps up and slashes me. I feel a burning sensation in my chest.

I am not about to let myself get torched twice. Backing

up, I raise my sword. While one opponent slinks away, the shorter one jumps up and clinks swords with mine. The sounds of metal hitting metal vibrate through the room as the two of us push back and forward, slashing at the air and at each other as we cross the room. We turn left, then right, then find ourselves nearing the corner of the room, but we keep going. We both seem too stubborn to accept defeat.

My opponent slashes me in the shoulder.

I hit her in the thigh.

She comes close to slashing my knees, and I jump out of the way.

I catch her on her hip, and she winces. As she staggers back into an armory closet, I slash my way forward 'til she's tucked inside its doors. I know I have her.

"Go, Gilly! Go, Gilly!" some of the girls shout.

I stick my sword under her chin. "Surrender."

"Never!" she shouts.

I falter as I vaguely recognize the voice, and that's where I lose ground. My opponent pushes on the door to the armory closet, and it almost hits me in the face. I stumble and fall as I jump out of the way. Within seconds, she has her foot on my back and her sword on my chin.

"I think you'll be the one surrendering," she says.

"Nice one, Cobbler," someone says, and I suddenly realize they're not referring to me.

Wait a minute.

"Anna?" I ask, sounding more out of breath than I'd like.

She pulls off her mask, and her long, shiny hair falls in ribbons down her back. Anna smiles haughtily. "In the flesh."

"Excellent!" Harlow applauds as she walks over to join us. "I didn't realize I had two Cobblers on this team."

Anna stands up and bows. "My Queen, I'm not on the team yet—but as you can see, I should be."

Harlow brightens at the queenie term of endearment. "How did you get the uniform?"

Anna looks up defiantly. "I took it from the armory so I could prove to you that I was a worthy opponent for anyone on this team—including my sister."

Whoa.

Jocelyn starts to laugh. "I like this Cobbler."

Harlow scratches her smooth chin and looks at us thoughtfully. "Me too." She points to Anna. "And this Cobbler is the clear winner of this battle. You're on the team."

"Yes!" Anna fist-bumps the girl she was with earlier. The girl removes her mask, and I see it's Gretel. *Great.*

Harlow looks at me. "And if you want to stay on this team, Gillian Cobbler, you better up your game. Everyone back to work!" She turns and walks away, and fencing practice resumes. My friends and even Gretel head off to work. Anna and I just stand there.

I extend my hand. "Well played."

Anna hesitates. Finally she shakes my hand and smiles.

"Was that so hard?" I ask.

"I still beat you," she points out, and I smile.

"You've had a lot of practice," I say. "We spent years playing pirates."

Anna's smile fades. "And you never let me win. Not even once. Why do you have to be better at everything?"

My face falls. "Is that what you think? That I'm better at everything?"

"I think no one really cares what I do," Anna says, and I try to interrupt. "Don't try to deny it. I'm only a year and a half younger than you, and I have eyes. Father and Mother think you're the golden girl in the boot. Our brothers and sisters think you're a hero. Even our teachers at Jack of All Trades fawn all over you. No one cares what Anna Cobbler does."

"Crumb cake, Anna. You're being ridiculous. Mother and Father love you."

"Maybe, but they don't make plans for me like they do you," Anna says. "All they talk about is you running the family business. *You can be trusted! You're a hero.*" She mimics my parents. "What about me? Father can't be bothered to listen when I talk about expanding Cobbler Shoes to include hosiery and hair accessories, like this one." Anna motions to an orange butterfly clip in her hair. With a quick tap, the butterfly clip springs to life and flaps its wings.

"That's so cool." I reach out to touch it. Anna pulls away.

"Father didn't think so." She sounds hurt. "He said, 'Ask Gilly what she thinks.'"

"I'm sure he didn't mean it like that," I say gently. I want to tell Anna the truth—that I don't even like working at Cobbler Shoes. It's not my dream. It's his and Anna's. But I can't find a way to say those words out loud.

"He doesn't care what I think, but I don't care anymore. Mr. Stiltskin thinks my accessories are genius, and he wants to help me manufacture them. I won't need to be part of

Cobbler Shoes. He says I'm so smart, I can have my own business."

My face tightens. "He's a trickster. You can't trust him."

"He said you'd say that," Anna says. "And he knows why you're here." A cold feeling sweeps over me. "This school—and me—we don't want or need a hero. We like Fairy Tale Reform School the way it is now. So do us all a favor and just go home, Gilly, before someone gets really hurt. I won't warn you again."

I don't go after her. I don't even know what I'd say. Does Anna really think Stiltskin is the only one looking out for her?

A sprite lands on my shoulder. "For you," she says, handing me a scroll.

I unravel it and read the message.

G—Royal Ladies-in-Waiting meeting tomorrow. Don't be late. (You're not getting out of this one!)

—Rapunzel

Happily Ever After Scrolls

Brought to you by FairyWeb—

Enchantasia's Number-One News Source!

Meet Fairy Tale Reform School's New Teacher: Rapunzel!

by Babette Babcock

Name: She is Princess Rapunzel to her loyal subjects, but according to her recently discovered brother, Jaxon, she is simply "Raz." Aww!

Occupation: With Princess Rose suffering from mental exhaustion while still under castle arrest, FTRS had no club advisor for their esteemed Royal Ladies-in-Waiting Club. Sources say Mr. Stiltskin wanted to cancel the group, but Rapunzel negotiated for the club to continue with her as advisor. "These girls have worked tirelessly on their princesses' behalf, and we're grateful for their dedication to Enchantasia," says Rapunzel.

Hobbies: Spending so many years in a tower has made this princess the most outgoing in the royal court. "I love to do anything and everything!" Rapunzel loves to draw and paint, but the princess also enjoys fencing and has recently taken up archery.

Strengths: Kick-butt businesswoman! Rapunzel's hair-care line is the most successful in the lands! Just don't call her a beauty. "I've got brains, and I'm not afraid to use them."

Weaknesses: Hates to be alone. "If you spent that many years in solitary confinement, you'd hate it too."

Check back for more coverage on Fairy Tale Reform School!

Chapter 10

Pink Ladies

As if my argument with Anna wasn't bad enough, now I have to go to a Royal Ladies-in-Waiting meeting!

This was a part of FTRS I did not miss.

As I sit in a pink satin chair, my head feels dizzy from the competing perfumes that cloud the air. Everywhere I look, I see my least favorite color: pink. Pink wallpaper, pink chairs, pink flowers, tablecloths, and teacups. Pink banners left over from Rose's delusional reign ("CHARMED to See You All Here!" they say in pink lettering) are being taken down by goblin student leader Tessa. Her bestie, Raza, has a new banner ready. "Welcome to the RLWs, Rapunzel!" it says in shimmery lilac.

I nudge Maxine. "No pink?"

"Of course not," she says in surprise and points to the purple necklaces that squeeze her thick neck. "Purple is Rapunzel's favorite color."

"Very good, Maxine!" compliments Tessa. I stare at her warily. She wasn't very nice to Maxine when I begged them to let Maxine join the club last semester. Tessa clears her throat. "I'm hoping the three of us can put bygones behind us. I could use all the help I can get in fixing the RLW reputation."

"From being known as brainwashed victims of Princess Rose?" I ask lightly.

Tessa's ears twitch. "We refer to it as being put under a spell that our poor princess was cursed with as well."

I snort. "Princess Rose was the one who *cast* the spell."

"Because Alva made her," Raza says. "It's all in the letter she sent us. Didn't you get one? She's recovering from the ordeal at her and the prince's lake house in Captiva. She feels dreadful about what happened."

I raise my eyebrows. "Does she? I guess having the delusional dream of taking control of the kingdom from your fellow princesses will do that."

"*Anyway*," Tessa says loudly—which is the approved way an RLW can change the subject without offending the other person (From the *RLW Handbook*, Rule 47, filed under "Perfectly Pink Conversations!"). "Rose will be as dewy as, well, a rose, when she returns to her duties next summer. In the meantime, we get Rapunzel."

At the mention of the princess's name, several girls begin brushing their hair with glittery gold brushes stamped with the letter *R*. They're part of Rapunzel's hair-care line.

I touch my hair. I didn't get to comb it this morning because Peaches ate my brush. When she coughed it up, it had turned into rock, which was different.

"Want me to fix your hair, Gilly?" Tessa asks brightly.

I back away. "No."

"You want to look your best for Rapunzel." She spins me around as I try to get away. "Don't be such a sprite about it. Let me just add a ribbon!" She unties a black-and-white ribbon from her wrist and pulls at my hair. I feel her tying the ribbon. "There!"

The girls in the room coo. One hands me a mirror. My brown hair has been pulled away from my forehead and the purple locks secured in the bow at the back of my head.

"From Rapunzel's accessories line," Tessa tells me. "Maybe she can bring us some items. We're not allowed packages anymore. Maybe if they're hidden in gardening supplies, Mr. Stiltskin won't notice."

"Gardening supplies?" Maxine asks.

"Yeah," Raza says. "Mr. Stiltskin had a bunch of RS members outside digging holes and testing soil yesterday. They planted a bunch of seeds." She shrugs. "Maybe gardening is going to be a new club."

Now what would that trickster be doing in the garden? Growing hay?

"Good afternoon, ladies."

We all jump to attention. Rapunzel has arrived with zero fanfare, unlike the princess welcomes we're accustomed to. Her waist-length blond hair is pulled back in a braid that is woven with purple ribbons. They match her floor-length dress, which is corseted with more ribbons. She makes eye contact with me, then quickly smiles at the group.

"Princess!" Tessa drops into a curtsy that we all quickly copy. "We are so honored to have you lead our humble RLW chapter."

"There is no need to curtsy," Rapunzel says, sounding embarrassed, "and please, don't call me Princess. I prefer Raz."

The RLWs look at one another in confusion.

A princess that doesn't want to be called a princess. This

is practically unheard of in Enchantasia. Rapunzel sounds as unpretentious as Jax.

She moves to the center of our group, and we all back up to give her gown space. "Before we get to business, I wanted to introduce our newest member."

"Newest member?" Tessa frantically consults her pink notebook, which is overflowing with sticky notes. "We haven't had a single pledge request."

I frown. Anna used to want to be in the RLWs, but I guess she hasn't pledged.

Rapunzel smiles. "This person came directly to me." She pulls a wand out of a hidden pocket and waves it at the back wall. A door appears. There are audible gasps as a boy enters the room.

"Ollie?" I blurt out. Maxine and I start to laugh.

"Ladies, that is rude," Rapunzel scolds, and we quickly stop.

"Thank you, My Princess." Ollie bows. "I expected there to be some hesitation. It's not every day a lad joins the Royal Ladies-in-Waiting."

"There's *never* a day that happens," says an elf sitting on a pink armchair. "This club is for girls." There's agreement among the group.

"Says who?" Rapunzel asks.

"Well, for starters, we're called the Royal *Ladies*-in-Waiting," Raza reminds her.

Rapunzel looks at Ollie and shrugs. "How do you know it's not really the Royal *Lads*-in-Waiting?" Ollie puffs out his chest and adjusts the shirtsleeves on his uniform. He's wearing pink cufflinks. "I don't believe clubs should discriminate based on gender or creature. That is not the RLW way."

Tessa and Raza begin stuttering. "No, but..."

"Us lads have as much to offer the royals as you lasses do," says Ollie, sounding a lot like a mini Blackbeard. "I would be honored to be this club's token male—for now."

"Excellent!" Rapunzel picks up the hem of her dress and glides around the room. "I like the idea of the RLWs changing with the times. Gone are the days when this club's sole purpose was just to do whatever was asked of you."

"But, Raz," says Tessa, trying the nickname on for size, "what if a royal does the asking?"

"You should question *anyone* who asks you to do something you don't feel comfortable with," she says, and I know immediately she is talking about not only Stiltskin, but also what happened with Princess Rose. "For too many years,

I accepted my sheltered fate and did nothing to try to change it. I assumed that the cards I had been dealt were meant to be, but I was wrong! Who said I had to be kept locked away? No one should decide your future for you but *you*. If you don't like where your life is headed, change it."

I start to applaud before I even realize what I'm doing.

"I like her," whispers Maxine.

"Me too." For so long, I thought I knew everything there was to know about the princesses. Rose may have fooled me, but my gut tells me Rapunzel is the real deal.

"Change takes time, but I think we can show the kingdom that the RLWs are capable of much more than turning napkins into swans," Rapunzel says. "This group can be anything we want it to be, so I want to hear your thoughts. What is an RLW to you?"

We look at her blankly. She waves her wand again. *Poof!* Quills and parchment appear on the tables around the room. "Let's get to work and decide," she says.

Inspired, we all run to grab a seat. Rapunzel stops me.

"May I have a word in the courtyard?" she asks.

Uh-oh. She's going to yell at me about crashing the royal ball. "Of course."

I glance at Maxine, but her tongue is hanging out of her mouth as she concentrates hard and presses the quill to the parchment. The quill breaks in half, but a new one magically appears and she starts again. I follow Rapunzel outside.

I swallow hard. "I just wanted to say I'm sorry for—"

"Shh!" Rapunzel sprinkles silver dust into her hands, then blows it into my face. I start to cough. "'Distraction dust," she says and places a small bag in my hand. "It can keep You-Know-Who from hearing our conversation for the next two minutes."

"Sweet." Maybe I'm not in trouble after all.

"Do you know what's not sweet?" Rapunzel says in a very unprincessy manner. "Crashing a party with foreign royals and causing such a scene that it lands on *Happily Ever After Scrolls*! If you had intel on what this menace was doing at FTRS, you should have shared it with the royal court. Not struck out on your own without a solid plan."

"I'm sorry. We didn't mean to ruin your party," I apologize. Princesses and their parties. Geez.

Rapunzel rolls her eyes. "I don't care about the party! It was just a cover so we could learn what he's been up to in other kingdoms. And you ruined our chance to find out!"

"We didn't know you were already onto him," I say in surprise. I always assume the royal court is two steps behind us.

"Do you really think we were going to allow a trickster like him to run FTRS?" Rapunzel sounds insulted. "Princess Ella agreed to let this school open because she liked Flora's vision for the students. But in the wrong hands, a gathering of kids like this could be used for evil. Look how Alva and Rose tried to control students!" Rapunzel shudders. "Stiltskin may claim he's trying to keep everyone here safe, but he must have an ulterior motive for choosing FTRS as his next stop. He certainly won't tell the royal court why he's here. He is refusing to meet with us."

"Did you learn anything at the party before the crash?" I ask meekly.

She sighs. "A bit. The Princess of Captiva told us he preyed on a similar school in her kingdom. She said he got students to help him with a 'special project' but to this day, she doesn't know what that project was. Some students became so loyal to him that they left town with him and haven't been seen since."

I feel ill. "My sister Anna is completely charmed by him,"

I confess. "She's a member of his Stiltskin Squad. What if she tries to follow Stiltskin when he leaves?"

Rapunzel looks me square in the eye as the distraction dust starts to fade. "You're the toughest girl I know. You've got to get through to her before it's too late. Find out what he's up to. If we work together, we can stop him."

I know Rapunzel is paying me a compliment, but I don't feel I deserve it. I'm not tough. If I were, I would have been able to talk sense into Anna already. She can't stand the sight of me. Neither can Flora, who seems to think I'm a failure. "FTRS isn't the same school it was when I was here the first time," I say sadly. "A lot of these kids *like* what Stiltskin is doing and don't want a hero to rescue them. I don't think I'm the best person to get through to Anna or anyone else right now. All I'm doing is spinning my wheels."

"This doesn't sound like the Gilly I've heard about from Jax," Rapunzel says. "He said you're someone who is always ready for a fight, and you don't quit 'til you win."

The last of the dust evaporates just like my hope. I smile grimly. "You can only win if you know the rules of the game."

Happily Ever After Scrolls

Brought to you by FairyWeb—

Enchantasia's Number-One News Source!

Rumpelstiltskin Challenges the Royal Court to a Bake-Off!

by Coco Collette

After taking their desire to meet with Mr. Stiltskin public in *HEAS*, the royal court has finally received an invite to Fairy Tale Reform School—for a bake-off. "I believe important discussions are more engaging when food is involved," says Mr. Stiltskin, who claims a security threat has kept him from opening the school's doors before now to anyone—including the royal court. "The students are very excited about this fun event. I plan on bringing my spatula-and-mixer A game, and the princesses should do the same."

"Mr. Stiltskin should know we have more important matters to discuss than frosting," says Snow White stiffly. "We won't be leaving the school grounds without answers." Parents have appealed to the princesses about school conditions. "We don't want another Alva situation," said one parent who learned in recent weeks that FTRS has stopped Pegasus Posts, put many school extracurriculars on hold, and canceled family visitation. Flora, who was always accessible to parents, has been silent.

Mr. Stiltskin says parents and the royal court have nothing to worry about. "They will see for themselves that all is well at FTRS," he says. "The students adore me and do everything asked of them. Isn't that why FTRS was created? To help turn misdirected criminals into obedient children? That's finally happening under my watch."

Check back for more coverage on the FTRS Bake-Off!

CHAPTER 11

I Want Candy

I wake up to the smell of cinnamon, chocolate—and something furry crawling on my legs. "Rodent!" I scream and push the covers away in a panic. "Oh. It's *you.*" My ridiculous mouse Fairy Pet squeaks madly. "How'd you get in here?" More squeaking. "Nope." I tug on my ear. "Can't understand you."

Peaches hops on my bed and quacks like crazy. Then she bites my big toe.

"Peaches!" Maxine scolds. "What do you mean, you stole Gilly's Fairy Pet from the classroom?" Peaches flaps. "What do you mean Gilly hasn't checked in on her mouse all week?"

All three of them—Peaches, the mouse, and Maxine—stare at me.

"How do you understand what that duck is saying?" I grumble.

"I listen." Maxine sniffs. "Peaches says she had to feed your mouse again since you forgot. You're supposed to stop in daily!" My mouse crawls over to Maxine and climbs in her hand. She feeds him a piece of leftover bread.

"I've been busy, okay? Rapunzel wants me to talk to Anna, and I can't get anywhere near her. She's always in class or with him, and no one will let me anywhere near his private kitchen. I even tried making an appointment with Stiltskin to try to butter him up and get in his club, but he wouldn't see me. I'm failing. Miserably."

"Well, that's no excuse to ignore... What is your mouse's name, anyway?"

"Who names a mouse?" I ask. The mouse starts to squeal at such a high volume that even Maxine winces and puts him down. We watch as the mouse scurries to a corner and drags back a piece of orange silk I recognize. I pick it up. "This is part of Anna's butterfly clip," I say in amazement. "How'd you get this?"

"Maybe your mouse has been spying on Anna too," Maxine marvels.

If he has, he's smarter than I gave him credit for. I let him crawl into my hand. "I guess a move like that deserves a name." I think for a moment. Anna once had an imaginary prince boyfriend named… "How about Wilson?" I ask, and the mouse seems to wag its long tail. It doesn't squeak. Maybe it likes it. "Okay, Wilson it is."

"Thank Wilson," Maxine whispers, nudging me, "for getting Anna's clip."

"You really want me to—" I stop myself. "Thanks, Wilson."

He squeaks for a moment, then tears a hole in Anna's butterfly wing. Maxine and I watch as the mouse sticks its nose in and pulls out a small, white pebble. We lean in to see what it is.

"Is that a rock?" Maxine asks.

"It's sort of soft like a bean. What's a bean doing in Anna's hair clip?"

Our bedroom mirror starts to glow bright blue. I hide Wilson behind my back.

"Good morning, Fairy Tale Reform School," Miri says. "Please finish your muffins and report to the former magic-carpet racing track that is now Stiltskin's Kitchen.

The royal court will be joining us within the hour. Students are required to wear the new FTRS uniforms. You will find them already hanging in your closets."

Maxine opens our closet. Two sparkly purple uniforms made of tulle and ball-gown material, along with sparkly gold stockings, a gold sweater, and heels hang on gold hangers. I reach for my blue uniform instead and watch as it shimmers and disappears.

"Fairy no!" I quickly grab my boots before they can be zapped away too. I pull the sweater off the rack and drop Wilson into the pocket. He'll have to hang with me 'til after the bake-off.

"One final note: Students who were assigned to speak to *Happily Ever After Scrolls* will find their approved, prewritten statements on their mini magical chalkboards. Headmaster Stiltskin would like to remind the rest of you not to speak to the royal court unless he orders you to do so. Those who attempt to tell *anyone* about matters at FTRS without his permission will face severe punishment. You have been warned." Miri clears her throat. "Have fun!"

Maxine and I look at each other. Stiltskin is hiding something. The question is: What?

***

Stiltskin's warning may have freaked us out, but the rest of FTRS seems excited about the bake-off. As we reach Stiltskin's Kitchen, there is already a line wrapped around the hallway to get in. Kids jump or fly out of the way as the hallway keeps trying to seal up and reappear in another place.

Ollie runs over to us. "Someone said Stiltskin is giving out free bags of Candy Wands and Genie Gummies!" He looks ridiculous in pale-green dress pantaloons and gold suspenders with a glowing, green bow tie. "Let's go get some!"

Harlow clears her throat as she breezes by with Kayla and Jocelyn. She's wearing a glittery black apron over a charcoal-gray beaded dress that must weigh fifty pounds. "Mr. Funklehouse, like the food here, the candy is off-limits to your group." Ollie frowns.

"But how can you let the other kids eat it?" Maxine asks worriedly.

Harlow shrugs. "There are no brains or beauties in that bunch." We glare at her, and she rolls her eyes. "Fairy be, don't be so bothered. Wolfington is already looking into potions to counteract whatever effects the candy gives off."

She begins to walk away, then looks at Jax and me and frowns. "Those uniforms are an abomination."

My jaw drops when our line weaves into the room. It looks like a candy factory exploded in here. The walls are covered in candy-patterned wallpaper, and candy-colored chandeliers dripping with candy hang from the ceiling. The floor has been transformed from stone to purple glass that screams Purple People Eater Licorice. In the center of the room, I spy several long tables with mixing bowls, magical mixers, spoons, and baking supplies. Ovens line the back wall, along with a large, candy-covered stopwatch.

"Bag?" says Gretel. She's chewing gum like a cow.

I step back. "No thanks. Candy is for suckers." Several kids behind me grab bags, then run to giant dispensers full of jelly beans, gummies, and Bubble Gum Mermaids, which I haven't seen in years.

Gretel pops a blue bubble in my face. "The headmaster said everyone has to take candy so… Take. The. Bag." She shoves it in my face.

I fold my arms across my chest. "I don't want his tainted candy."

"Han!" Gretel shouts, and I notice something in her

pocket—a packet of seeds. What are those for? "The problem sister thinks she's too good for the headmaster's candy."

Hansel stalks over with a face as grim as his sister's.

"Candy is no good for you," I say. "My mother never let us have it." I reach for Gretel's shirt hoping to swipe the seeds. "You have some chocolate on you." She steps out of my reach.

"You never had candy because you couldn't afford it," Hansel sneers. "Your sister has it all the time when we're with the headmaster."

"That explains a lot," Ollie mumbles.

Hansel stands over him. He's twice Ollie's size. "Got a problem, pirate?"

"Hey, you called me pirate!" Ollie beams. "I appreciate that."

Hansel nudges him. "Take the candy. *Now.*"

"We don't want to be brainwashed into his Stiltskin Squad, okay?" Kayla says.

Hansel rolls his eyes. "*Please.* You, fairy, are seconds from being tossed out of this place and turned into a tree like the rest of your family."

Kayla lunges at him, but Jax holds her back. How does Hansel know about Kayla's family? What else has Stiltskin told him?

"I'll make them take sweets," says Hayley, running over. "You guys should go deal with that riot at the Giant Gummies table."

Hayley points to Anna, who looks overwhelmed as kids in her line freak out about a jammed gummy machine. Kids are throwing punches, and illegal magic is swirling in the air. My instinct is to help her, but when she catches my eye, it's clear that's the last thing she wants. I stay put, and Hansel and Gretel rush over.

Hayley hands us bags. "Haven't you guys learned how to deal with the RS yet? *Pretend* to do what they want. Take the candy, and when no one is looking, dump it." She shows us her sweater pocket. It's full of gum.

"Who are you?" Jocelyn asks snippily.

"I'm in your Magical Fairy Pets class," Hayley says. "Your cat ate my unicorn's breakfast."

Trumpets sound, and everyone looks to the doorway. My jaw drops as Mr. Stiltskin rides into the room on a horse, waving and throwing candy as kids scream like he's the lead singer of Gnome-More. He's certainly dressed like a rocker in a gold glitter ensemble that has the initials RS lit up on the back of his jacket. He looks briefly our way before focusing on the teachers who have gathered on the other side of the room. Madame Cleo is being beamed in from a large silver mirror in Blackbeard's dirty hands.

"Good morning!" Stiltskin steps off the horse with help from his squad. He quickly climbs onto a throne-like chair. "I'm so lucky to be loved by this school!" he says, looking at a *Happily Ever After Scrolls* reporter. The woman scribbles furiously on her parchment while a second piece of parchment and second quill write on their own. "Who is excited for today's bake-off?" he asks, and kids scream. "I know Professor Flora is excited to be our judge. Tough job though. I wouldn't want to choose between my *boss* and the royals in a bake-off." He laughs, but Flora's expression is hard to read.

"Sir?" Miri's voice is extra-loud in the large room. "They're here."

Stiltskin leans back in his chair lazily. "Children, please take your seats and show our royal court how well you've learned to listen under my guidance." My classmates practically run to their rugs as his RS squad watches. Even the mer-kids stop swishing their tails and stay still in their tanks. "Excellent! Show them in."

The trumpets sound again, and a group of royal guards

precede Rapunzel, Ella, and Snow. Each princess looks more beautiful than the next in gowns covered by cream-colored aprons that are stitched with the words *Royals Rule*. The three princesses move around the room, shaking hands. Finally they make their way to Stiltskin. He steps off his throne and shakes their hands. He looks taller than normal. It makes me wonder if he bewitched his shoes to give himself more height.

"Thank you for coming," he says. "I am sad to see Princess Rose is not with you."

"She's still recovering," says Ella coolly as she walks over to Flora. "It's good to see you, Stepmother. I've been worried about you. It's not like you to give FTRS to someone else to rule without consulting me first."

"Now, now, Flora is an adult. Some deals are hers alone to make," Rumpelstiltskin says as Flora looks awkwardly at the floor. He quickly changes the subject. "So let's bake! Princesses, what will you be making?"

"Rapunzel and I are making a blueberry cobbler," Princess Ella says.

"I am making an apple pie," Snow says wryly and looks at Harlow. "I do hope the Evil Queen will have a piece."

Harlow looks amused. "With pleasure."

"And I'm making raspberry boysenberry rhubarb tarts," Mr. Stiltskin says as he fires up his mixer and waves a wand at the large clock on the back wall. "The bake-off begins now!"

The students around me begin to cheer wildly. I suspect their enthusiasm is from a combination of the sugar they've just consumed and whatever magic-altering ingredients Stiltskin added. I glance at Anna and the RS squad, talking on the side of the room. Gretel and a few others have packs of seeds in their hands. Han whistles softly, and I see Stiltskin look up. He quickly nods, and some of the RS members start to leave the room together.

"Should we follow them?" Jax asks, nudging me.

"We'll get in trouble," I say, thinking of what Anna will do if she spots me.

"When has that ever stopped you before?" Jocelyn whispers.

I hesitate. "I know, but Anna doesn't want me to bother her."

"So?" Kayla asks. "That didn't stop you from going after me when you knew I was in over my head. Anna is in trouble. So is everyone else here, and if we don't do something to help them, they're going to live in a candy-coated 'I Heart Stiltskin' world forever."

"But we have no idea what he's planning or how to stop it,"

I say helplessly. I feel Wilson stick his head out of my pocket. He's got the bean in his mouth. He drops it, and Jax picks it up.

"Is this what I think it is?" Jax holds it up. "Where'd you get a magic bean?"

"Magic bean?" we repeat a little too loudly. Kids nearby shush us.

"It was in Anna's hair clip," Maxine says. "Gilly's mouse found it."

"These are banned," Jax says, sounding nervous. "If one was planted, and it grew to full height, it would give the giants access to Enchantasia. They could snuff out the whole country with one giant step. Why does Anna have one, and where did she find it?"

My heart starts to pound. Anna may not want me to interfere, but if she's messing with magic beans, she's jeopardizing our whole family and this kingdom. I can't let Stiltskin get away with that. We need to know what is going on. "We have to break into his office."

Ollie pats me on the back. "Glad to see you've come to your senses, thief. Now how do we get out of here without being seen?"

"You need a distraction," Hayley says, and I am startled

when I realize she's heard our whole conversation. "Let me help you get him."

I stop and look at Hayley for a moment, considering the risk.

"Please," she says.

I think back to the Magical Fairy Pets class where she talked about how much she missed her family. A hero never works alone, I remind myself. "Okay," I say and she grins. "What's our plan?"

"I've already got one. Go with it," Kayla says, and her wings pop out of her back. She flies across the room and points to Stiltskin. "This man is a liar! He stole my family, and he won't tell me what he's done with them! He's holding us all captive here!"

"She's creating a distraction all right," Jax says. "Everyone slowly make your way backward out of the room."

Mr. Stiltskin looks furious. "I don't know what you're talking about. This child has clearly had too much candy. See the dispensers I placed throughout the room? The students love how I treat them, right?" Kids cheer.

Snow shuts off her mixer. "I hope so. Because if this child is telling the truth, you have some explaining to do. Are you neglecting students?" The *HEAS* reporter runs forward, her parchment and quill floating along beside her.

Flora moves toward Kayla, but Stiltskin pulls her back. "Absolutely not! Look how well I feed them! I'm not neglecting anyone. Someone please escort this child to the infirmary. She's clearly ill."

"I'm not sick!" Kayla says as two RS members approach her. "I want answers! Where is my mother? Why won't you give my sisters back? What kind of deal did you make with them?" She looks at the royal court. "He turned my mother and sisters into trees, and I have no clue why. I want to know what happened and how to get them back!" She bursts into tears, and my heart breaks.

Kayla might be doing what she can to give us a getaway, but her pain is real. I hesitate, not wanting to leave her, but Jax tugs on my arm as we reach the doorway. As we slip down the hall, I can still hear Stiltskin talking.

"Take her away," he says gruffly. "I'm sorry for the interruption, everyone. That child is obviously too sick to stay at FTRS. I'll see to it that she is transferred elsewhere immediately."

Chapter 12

The Break-In

The halls are empty as we slip through one hallway after another, trying to find our way to Stiltskin's office, but we keep getting turned around.

"This place is more of a maze than ever!" Ollie groans as we jump through a new doorway and land next to the wand-training room again. Two new hallways open up, and we stare at them warily. "We've been down this hallway three times! We're never going to find our way to his office."

"It's like he's put the hallway monitor on the fritz so that no one can go anywhere but the bake-off," Hayley suggests. "Pretty clever."

"Where do you think they took Kayla?" Maxine asks worriedly. "Do you think he's really going to kick her out of school?"

"My sister won't let him," Jocelyn says defiantly. "If she has to, she'll hide Kayla with cloaking spells, but I don't think she'll have to. The teachers won't let her be kicked out. Even Flora wouldn't go for that."

"I hope you're right," I say grimly. "Kayla stood up to Stiltskin for the greater good. All I've done since I arrived is tick off Anna. Maybe I'm really just a washed-up hero."

"Is this about what Stiltskin said to you?" Jax asks.

"Flora basically said the same thing," I remind him. "I don't know what I'm doing anymore. I feel like I'm spinning my wheels."

"Then stop spinning!" Maxine yells at me and I blink. Maxine never yells. Not at me. "Since when do you listen to what others say? Especially someone like Stiltskin, a big ol' baddie who is brainwashing your sister and must have poor Flora under some sort of gag order. The Wicked Stepmother believes in you. She just can't say it out loud. Trust your gut and know what's right. We believe in you, even if you don't believe in yourself."

The others nod. I smile. "Okay. I guess I better start pulling my weight."

"That's the thief we know and love," Jax teases. "Let's find some clues to get out of this maze."

I look around. Every hall in this drafty castle has the same gray stone walls, oil paintings done by students, motivational signs (Why Be Wicked When You Can Be Wonderful Instead?), and mirrors. There are actually *loads* of mirrors that Miri can spot us in. Why she hasn't shown up yet to yell at us, I'm not sure.

Jax pulls one of the torches off the wall and peers down a darkened, empty hallway. "Let's go this way."

"That's the observatory, Prince," Jocelyn says. "Can we do this my way? He won't notice a teensy bit of magic when he's busy baking." She blows a puff of smoke, and purple smog lays a trail down a new hall.

I start to follow but feel squirming in my sweater pocket. Wilson pops his head out and begins to squeak like mad. I think he's trying to warn us about something. He squeaks louder, and that's when I see it shining in a small gap in the ceiling—a dagger. "Get out of that hall! It's a trap!"

A rumbling sound rocks the hallway. Wilson and I watch as the ceiling opens, revealing a row of daggers. Jax, Jocelyn, Hayley, and Maxine come running back, but Ollie is still behind them. Maxine and I scream as Ollie slides toward us, barely making it out of the hall before a dagger shoots into the floor, pinning his coat.

"Guess this means I have to go back to my old uniform," Ollie jokes, sounding out of breath. He shrugs out of it, and Jocelyn makes the coat disappear with a wave of her hand. "How'd you know it was a trap?"

"Wilson warned me," I say, surprised myself. I give him a treat from my pocket, and the mouse nibbles it.

"Of course he did." Hayley leans in and listens to the mouse's squeals. "He said the only hall that will lead to the office is the one on the left. The rest are booby-trapped."

"You can understand him?" I ask.

Hayley blushes and spritzes herself with water. "It's sort of my gift," she says shyly. "I guess I should come clean. The truth is I'm part mermaid, and mermaids can talk to other animals."

"Is that why you're always doing that water-spritzing thing?" Jocelyn asks. "Because it's rather odd." Maxine nudges her. "No offense."

"I get parched if I go too long between baths," Hayley explains. "I don't want Stiltskin to know what I really am. He's not a huge fan of mermaids."

"Or fairies, witches, or sprites," Jocelyn adds. "Get in line."

"We'd never tell him," I say, and Hayley smiles. "Let's

get in that office. If Wilson says this is the hall, then this is the hall."

We slip into the new hall before it shimmers and disappears. There are no elves on cleaning duty or wayward students on their way to the dorms. The school feels creepy this empty. A new hall begins to waffle in front of us and we dive through it, landing in the castle foyer where discarded signs, confetti, and the red carpet from the princesses' arrival still cover the floor.

"Yes!" Ollie cheers.

Jocelyn rushes to the oak doors of Rumpelstiltskin's office. She runs her hand along the large, gold lock, then conjures a purple fireball. "Step back. I got this."

"Wait!" I shout, but I'm too late. Jocelyn's magic bounces off the lock and sends us flying backward, where we land in a heap along the back wall. Wilson sticks his head out of my pocket, looking dizzy. "Your magic won't work on his door! He probably has protection charms all over to keep anyone from breaking in."

Hayley lies on her back and stares at the ceiling. "Maybe he has a hideaway key hidden somewhere nearby."

"Fish face, Stiltskin isn't dumb enough to keep a spare key outside his office," Jocelyn snaps.

"That was rude!" Maxine tells her. "Apologize."

"Guys?" Ollie says as they argue. "Look!" He is standing in front of Stiltskin's open door waving a set of keys. "Skeleton keys," he says with glee. "A pirate's best friend for thieving. Now come on. We don't have all day."

We pile into the office. It looks just like it did when Jax and I were here. The fire is blazing. Stiltskin's desk is bare and gleaming. His chair is tucked under his desk.

"Neat freak," Jax says and tugs on a few office drawers. We peer into them, staring into nothingness. "No quills, no parchments, no school documents. Where is he hiding his things?"

Jocelyn opens his file cabinet. "Nothing here either. He travels light."

"Or he doesn't plan on staying long," I say.

"I doubt we're that lucky." Ollie begins stomping around the room. "He's just a good hider. But he's no match for a pirate used to keeping things below floorboards." He stops and hits one spot again. I hear it echo. "We've got a winner!"

Jax crouches down, and we roll back a red oriental rug. There is a small door underneath, but it's locked. I feel Wilson wiggle out of my pocket and run down my arm. He's clearly on a mission so I put him down next to Jax. Wilson sniffs the lock, then squeezes himself through the keyhole. Seconds later, we hear a click, and Jax opens the door. "This mouse of yours is pretty smart."

Maybe a mouse isn't such a bad fairy pet after all. "Yes, he is. Good boy, Wilson." The mouse sniffs the air, and I toss him another treat.

We peer into the darkness below. Maxine pulls a bag out of her pocket. "Illuminating pixie dust," she tells us and dumps the contents into the hole. The dust lights up the area below. Jagged rocks in the ground drip with condensation, and cold air rises into the room. "I can't tell how deep it goes back, but it looks like it's empty."

"Drop me in, and I'll poke around," Ollie says, shimmying into the small hole. Wilson disappears in after him. We lean over the edge to look.

"See anything?" Hayley asks.

"There's some hay on the floor, but the hole is empty. Wait! There's a small jar down here." He jingles it. "It's filled with beans." Jax and I look at each other.

"Magic beans," Jax whispers. "Ollie, bring them up. We have to get them out of here before anyone tries to use them."

"*Eeeeeeeeeeeee!*"

We hear a high-pitched whistling sound and hold our ears. The sound is so painful that no one can move. I manage to open my eyes and look around the room. An antique alarm clock on the mantel is buzzing so loudly that it shakes and falls off the fireplace. I reach out and grab it just before it hits the ground.

"Your time is half up!" a voice inside the clock whispers. "Pay up or pay the price. Pay up or pay the price..."

"Who is that?" Hayley asks anxiously.

I hold the clock up to the light and try to read the letters etched into the back. *JA.* "I don't know," I say.

Boom!

The door to the office flies off its hinges, knocking me onto my butt. Anna, Hansel, and Gretel come bursting through the door, followed by Stiltskin. When he catches sight of the open trapdoor and the clock in my hands, his skin turns almost violet.

"Seize them!" he shouts and waves his wand at us.

"No!" I hear Anna shout, but she can't get to me in time. Stiltskin's spell sucks my friends and me up into a vortex, pulling us out of the room and dropping us into cold, dark waters. A scream barely escapes my lips before I begin to sink into the icy waters below. Then the world around me fades to black.

CHAPTER 13

Stormy Seas

I feel a shock and come to seconds later as an electric eel nips at my boots. That's when I remember: I'm in the *water*! My body continues to sink and I try to kick up, but my ridiculous outfit is weighing me down. I quickly pull at the heavy skirt, unlooping some of the ribbons and yanking it off so that only a leotard remains. I slip out of my sweater too, and momentarily panic about Wilson. Then I remember he escaped into the trapdoor with Ollie. He's safe—for now.

I look around as bubbles escape my nose. I have to get to the surface before I run out of air, but it's so dark I can't tell which way is up. A coral reef lies to my left along with what appears to be a cave. Sea grass sways below me, and I feel my foot get tangled in a long vine. I furiously shake myself free and try not to freak out. That's when I see a long, black cape sinking into the darkness. *Jocelyn.*

I kick my way through the murky water to reach her. Her eyes are closed as I rip off her cape and heavy skirt. I hang on to her and try to figure out my next move. That's when I hear pounding. I look up and see Jax hitting what looks like a glass ceiling as sleek gray creatures surround him. *Sharks.* I want to scream and warn him, but I can't. My lungs feel like they are on fire. My heart is pounding in my chest. Jocelyn is still unconscious. I have no clue how we're getting out of here. That's when I hear more banging. Through the reeds, I spot Maxine kicking at something invisible in front of her. I grab Jocelyn's arm and pull her with me toward Maxine, and that's when I hit an invisible wall of glass. Suddenly I know where we are.

We're *in* Madame Cleo's tank, but I don't see the sea witch.

Holding on to Jocelyn, I use my free hand to join Maxine in pounding the glass. I've seen it break before when I was in detention. We pound desperately, panic rising in my chest as a school of fish swims by me. That's when I see him standing in the center of the room with a smug smile on his face. Rumpelstiltskin.

He shows no signs of remorse as he watches us fight for

our lives. The dark water makes it hard to see, but I wonder if Anna is with him and if she's trying to do anything to stop this madness. With my last breath, I hit the wall with all my strength. It does nothing. My eyes start to drift closed, and Maxine begins to sink beside me. I grab her arm with my other hand. Soon we're all descending into the darkness.

Zap!

A shock of light behind us makes my eyes flutter open. I feel someone's hands on me, and then something cold is pressed against my lips. Air fills my lungs. I can breathe! Whatever this thing is, it's giving me oxygen. I watch as a mermaid places the same object on Jocelyn's, Jax's, and Maxine's lips, and they slowly start to come to. Then I realize who I'm looking at. It's Hayley in her mermaid form! Her hair is pale blue, like her new fishtail. Her yellow eyes are so mellow that I feel suddenly calm. She squeezes my hand, and I notice her fingers are webbed. Then she motions to the mermaid beside her.

Madame Cleo does *not* look calm. Her hair is fiery orange, and her face is almost white with rage as she lets out an ear-splattering scream I've only heard her do once before. Rumpelstiltskin steps away from the tank as the glass begins to splinter. I watch Cleo and Hayley swim away, and then, suddenly, there is a flash of light and I see Professor Harlow burst into the room with Wolfington and Blackbeard. She summons the breaking glass toward her, and my friends and I get sucked into a wave of water that pours into the detention room. Members of the RS squad get swept away in the surge of water, but Stiltskin manages to grab hold of a chandelier. Just as quickly, the leak is plugged with a wave of Harlow's hand.

I cough violently and take in huge gasps of air. Jax coughs up a small fish, and Maxine is shivering beside Jocelyn. Ollie appears with warming blankets that he wraps around each of us.

"How...did...you...know...where...to...find...us?" Maxine asks him.

I see Wilson poke his head out of Ollie's pocket. "One of the RS members cracked and told me where you were being sent."

Anna? I mouth, and he nods.

She tried to save me.

"Once I knew where you were, I alerted Miri to let Madame Cleo know, but Hayley was already with her," Ollie says.

"Oh, darlings, are you all right?" Madame Cleo says

from inside the tank. Hayley swishes alongside her. "We came as quickly as we could. We had to stop for coral hearts first. Hayley and I didn't think you had enough oxygen left to survive 'til the glass broke."

"That girl is half mermaid?" Rumpelstiltskin says with disgust as he swings from the chandelier. An RS member runs underneath, and Stiltskin drops into his arms and hops to the ground. He glares at Hayley.

"She might be, but the others aren't!" Professor Harlow cries, rushing to Jocelyn to check on her. "Humans can't survive that long underwater!"

"And ye could have hurt my lass, ye scallywag!" Blackbeard points his sword at Stiltskin.

His RS squad rushes in to protect him. Anna locks eyes with me. She doesn't say anything, but she looks relieved to see I'm okay.

"Darling, I'm fine," Madame Cleo says, and her hair turns red.

"You see? She's fine," Stiltskin says calmly. "Now lower your sword, Professor Blackbeard, or we'll be taking it from you along with your job." Blackbeard puts his sword back into its holster reluctantly.

"Let me through!"

Flora rushes into the room with Kayla behind her. Flora's face crumples when she sees us, and Kayla starts to cry. "So it's true? You placed these students in Cleo's tank? You could have killed them, you monster!"

Stiltskin chews on a strand of licorice in his hand. "I'm headmaster, and I'll dole out punishments as I see fit." Flora's face darkens. "They were trespassing on my private property and needed to be reprimanded." He glances at Kayla. "Disobedient children cannot be rewarded. They should be dealt with accordingly."

"They're children!" Flora shouts. "You went too far. Threatening to expel Kayla, hurting the others—I want you to leave Fairy Tale Reform School at once!"

"Finally, she's come to her senses," Harlow mutters.

Stiltskin waves his wand, and a long contract appears in his hands. "Temper, temper, Professor Flora. This is no longer your school, remember? It's mine." He smiles with glee. "At *my* school, children who break into the headmaster's office must pay."

"We know what you're hiding," I say, my teeth chattering. "You stole magic beans." I watch Stiltskin's expression change.

"Is this true?" Wolfington asks. "Magic beans are outlawed in Enchantasia. The consequences of just one bean being planted could be disastrous!"

Stiltskin stares at me. "So where are these supposed magic beans I have?"

I look down. "They disappeared when you sent us into Madame Cleo's tank."

He laughs. "See? Lies! All lies! Even if I do own beans, who says they're magic? You? The little hero?" he mocks. "Well, you're not a hero any longer. You couldn't even save yourself in that tank. Accept it, Gillian Cobbler. Your shining moment has passed. No one—including your sister—needs you anymore."

"That's not true," I say angrily. "Maybe the kids here don't see it, but what you're doing at FTRS is wrong, and I don't have to be a hero to know you don't belong here." Maxine smiles at me encouragingly.

"Get them out of here," Stiltskin says, looking pointedly at Anna. She takes my arm.

"*No!*" Flora shouts, and Anna drops it. "You may have tricked me into giving you this school, but I won't allow you to continue to hurt my students. I know why you took Kayla's family, and I know the beans you have in your possession are real, and you will—"

"I've listened to enough," Stiltskin says. "Be gone!" With a wave of his hand, Flora's body begins to shimmer. Flora reaches out to stop him, but it's no use. Kayla jumps back as Flora's skin turns ashy gray, then hardens into stone. The Wicked Stepmother is now nothing more than a statue. I cry out, but there is no sound.

"No!" Kayla screams.

There is a sudden barrage of shouting and screaming as my professors surround Stiltskin. With a wave of his wand, they're all thrown back.

"Remember who calls the shots around here," Stiltskin says viciously. "You all work for *me*! It was part of Flora's contract." The document appears again as if by magic, and Wolfington and Blackbeard look it over. "And my deals are never broken unless I want them to be!" He laughs wickedly.

I glance at Anna and then at Flora's statue. How many more people will he hurt before someone takes him on? I don't know if I have it in me, but I have to try. "What will it take to get you to leave FTRS and never come back?" I blurt out. The others look at me.

"You want to make a deal, Cobbler?" His smile fades. "Better think before you make one—that was Flora's mistake. You only get one shot."

"Cobbler," Harlow warns with a growl. "Don't!"

My mouth feels dry. "I know what I want," I say and glance at my friends. "I just need a moment to compose my thoughts." I walk over to the others, who are just starting to stand up. I can't do this without them. I know now a hero is only as strong as the people she surrounds herself with. We're a team. We huddle into a group.

"I'm sorry," I whisper. "I just couldn't take it anymore."

"I'm proud of you." Maxine gives my hand a squeeze. "Whatever the deal is, I'm in too. We can do this if we work together."

Ollie nods. "You know I'm always ready for a good fight."

"I'll do anything to get rid of those beans," Jax adds.

"Let's get this guy," Jocelyn agrees.

"Me too." Kayla touches my hand. "Just please make sure this deal involves me getting my family back too, okay?" I nod.

"Time's a-wasting, Miss Cobbler!" Stiltskin sings. "Do you want a deal or not?"

I look at my friends. "So you guys are in with me?"

Jax grins. "'Til the end. Go get 'em."

I turn around. "We want a deal. We'll sign it together."

"No!" Harlow cries again. "Jocelyn, what are you thinking?" Jocelyn doesn't answer.

"Miss Cobbler, please reconsider," says Wolfington.

Stiltskin snaps his fingers, and a large parchment appears. "Too late. She asked for a deal, and a deal she'll get. So what do you all want?"

I think for a moment, then look at Jax. "Flora created FTRS to make us better people, and FTRS isn't the same without her in charge. I want you to give the school back to her, give Kayla back her family—in their original fairy form—and for you to leave this school and never return. And I want Anna released from FTRS."

"Gilly, that isn't your call to make!" Anna snaps.

Stiltskin scratches his chin. "She's right. Anna is the only one who can decide her fate. But you can have that troublemaker, Kayla, and the fish." He looks at Hayley in disgust. "I don't want more of her kind here."

"I wouldn't stay if you paid me," comes Hayley's voice loud and clear from inside the tank. "I'll go wherever Gilly leads me." Cleo applauds her.

"It may be to your death." Stiltskin smiles. "In fact, I'm sure we won't see your faces around here again." I stay stoic. "Your deal should be specific, Cobbler. What else do you want?"

I swallow. "I want Kayla's family brought to the school grounds," I add. "You can move trees, I'm sure. Prove to me that they're here, and that way I'll know for sure you'll take care of them."

He laughs to himself and then waves his hand. "Done." He points to the mirror on the wall, and I see an image of the grounds where three trees now stand.

Kayla flies to the mirror and touches it. "That's them! I can feel it."

"Anything else?" Stiltskin asks.

I glance at my friends. Flora returned to headmaster, Stiltskin out of our school, Kayla's family returned, Anna home and safe. He hasn't agreed to that last part, but I know I can change Anna's mind. "That's it."

"Now you have to listen to what I want," Stiltskin says. "That's part of the deal. I get something too, or the deal is off." He smiles evilly. "Bring me a golden goose."

"A golden goose?" I repeat. Isn't that the one I read about

in the papers the night Anna was sentenced? "I thought it was a myth."

"It's real, I assure you," Stiltskin says. "The golden goose lives deeps in the Hollow Woods and lays eggs of the purest gold there is." His eyes narrow. "I *want* that goose. If you get it, all that you ask for will be yours. Understood?"

My friends and I look at each other and nod. "We understand."

Stiltskin snaps his fingers, and a quill appears. He taps the parchment and motions for us to sign. I hear Anna inhale sharply. "Sign and I'll let you be on your way at first light."

My eyes quickly scan the calligraphy written in tiny print. There isn't time to read it, but I know that I need to take this deal. I pull the quill from his hands and sign my name in loopy script. I hand it to Jax who does the same, then passes it down the line as Harlow continues to yell at us. When Jocelyn is finished writing the last signature, the parchment glows bright yellow, then disappears with a pop.

"Excellent," Stiltskin says. "We have a deal."

Happily Ever After Scrolls

Brought to you by FairyWeb—

Enchantasia's Number-One News Source!

The Votes Are *Not In*. Rumpelstiltskin's Bake-Off with the Royal Court Ends in Tie

by Coco Collette

The bake-off between the Fairy Tale Reform School headmaster and the royal court was a lively one with much cheering from the candy-loving students at FTRS. "Stiltskin is the clear winner," said Rosaria Romena, a new student at FTRS sent there for talking back to her teachers at Fairy Yours School. "His sweets are sweet!"

Rosaria may have picked a winner, but Flora, the school's former headmistress, was not on hand to break the tie. Flora rushed out of the proceedings when an alarm went off in the building, and Mr. Stiltskin said she was too tied up to return. "I'm sure she would have chosen my tarts as the clear winner. I guess we'll have to do this again soon to find out!"

The royal court did not seem happy with the outcome. After the alarm, Mr. Stiltskin was called away as well and needed to cancel his meeting with them. "We are not sure what game Mr. Stiltskin thinks he's playing, but as the governing body in Enchantasia, our concerns will not be ignored," said Ella. "We want answers about what's going on at Fairy Tale Reform School."

"They may control the land, but I control this school," Stiltskin said when questioned. He pointed to a binding contract Flora signed as proof of his leadership. "Flora herself would tell you that."

But in order to ask Flora, we'd have to find her. Miri, the school spokesmirror, wouldn't comment, but sources tell us Flora hasn't been seen since the bake-off. Her daughters told the Dwarf Police Squad that they could not find their mother when they returned to FTRS for their Saturday night dinner with her. "If anyone has seen our mother, we urge them to come forward," said Dahlia tearily. "We fear she may be in trouble."

CHAPTER 14

A Fine Mess

Fiddlesticks, this is awkward. As we sit at Professor Harlow's long, candlelit dinner table, I can hear pots and pans being thrown while Harlow yells at the top of her lungs.

"Of all the foolish, selfish things to do, she had to suggest they sign a contract with Rumpelstiltskin!" Harlow shouts, and another pot hits a wall. "One she didn't read!" I hear someone whispering. "No, that's not it at all! It's like that child has a death wish! They won't find the golden goose. It's a myth! Gottie, Alva, and I tried to find it for years! They're goners in those woods!"

Maxine slurps her first course noisily. "Wow, this soup the Evil Queen made is delicious—*cough!* Is that paprika I taste in the—" She starts hacking so bad Kayla has to hand her a glass of water.

"Does she sentence *just* herself to a foolish quest?" Harlow asks. "Nooo! She convinces my sister and those other delinquents to sign on with her!"

Jocelyn lights and extinguishes a candle in front of her with a wave of her hand. "Wow, and I thought my sister hated you before, Cobbler. Nice job."

"Jocelyn, maybe you could do something constructive instead of making digs at Gilly," Jax suggests. A book about geese habitats is open in front of him. Wilson sits on the open pages, seemingly reading. "We only have a few hours left before we head out."

"And we still have a lot to do so everyone, please pitch in," Kayla says, her eyes glued to a stack of Enchantasia history books. After checking that the trees outside school really were her mother and two sisters, she came straight to Harlow's chambers to start researching the golden goose. She's so intent on finding it that she's given everyone research to do. Jocelyn is supposed to work on protection spells for our journey. Ollie is using a crystal on a map of the Hollow Woods to try to find the goose's location as Maxine takes notes with a self-writing quill, and Jax is tracking goose behaviors. Even Peaches is walking across Harlow's gothic table, eating silverware and coughing up things like quills and magic wands, while Jax studies her every move. Ducks and geese are definitely related, but I don't think any animal is like Peaches.

I'm supposed to be reading a stack of *HEAS* that include stories on the mythic goose, but it's hard to concentrate. Another loud crash from the kitchen makes me jump.

"She wasn't smart enough to ask Stiltskin to send us on this fool's errand with her either, so now they must face the Hollow Woods alone!" Harlow continues to yell. "She's as bullish as Flora…and look where she wound up. In the dungeon as a statue!" I wince. "With all the protection spells on this castle, we can't even send aid to them if we want to! They'll probably get eaten by giants when they pass the first fairy stream!"

"What fairy stream?" Ollie says worriedly and taps the crystal on the map. "I don't see one on here. Is this map even up-to-date?"

I feel like the walls are closing in on me. "I'm going to take a walk and clear my head." I leave Harlow's dining room and walk down the hall to the dungeon. Flora's statue is next to the one of Alva. Flora is frozen in mid-argument, her arms outstretched, trying to save us.

"I'm so sorry," I whisper.

"So am I," I hear someone say, and I turn around. Anna walks out of the shadows, still wearing her glittery RS school uniform. Since ours got ruined in Cleo's tank, we got our old ones back. My basic blue romper looks so different next to Anna's shiny new dress.

Her hair is pulled back in a long braid like Rapunzel's, and I spot something green and ivory pinned in her hair.

"Is that the dragon's tooth comb, I got you for your birthday?" I ask.

"*Stole*," Anna corrects me. She pulls it out of her hair. "Pete took it back, but when I saved up enough money, I went to Combing the Sea and rebought it."

"You did?" My heart feels like it might burst. "That's the Anna I know and love."

Anna sighs. "Gilly, that Anna was miserable."

"What do you mean?" I ask.

"At home, at school, in the village, everyone just wanted me to be a mini you, and I'm not," Anna says. "I don't know who I am yet, but I know I like being part of a squad that cares about my opinion." She smiles shyly. "I'm happy here. That's what I came here to tell you. I know you're worried about me, but don't be. I'm learning so much from Stiltskin."

My face darkens. "I don't believe that. He's evil, Anna."

"He's not," she insists. "You just have to get to know him. I really do hope you can find that golden goose and help Flora—she always seemed nice—but I came here to tell you not to ask me to leave again because I won't. I'm staying here with him." I start to protest. "No, listen to me. Father is never going to give me his business. He wants you to run it. And I want to be more than someone's sidekick."

"I'd never make you a sidekick," I fire back. "That's what Stiltskin is doing. How can you be so blind?"

"I'm not going to do this with you again," Anna says. "I know you don't like him, but I do. You have to let me try to figure out my own way." She hesitates, then reaches out and hugs me.

I'm surprised, but I hug her back and don't let go.

"I love you, Gilly," she whispers. "Good luck out there."

"Thanks." I am not sure what to say. "Just promise me

you'll remember one thing while I'm gone: you don't have to do this."

Anna pulls away. We stare at each other for a moment, then she hurries up the stairs. I watch her go.

"It's hard to accept that not everyone wants the same things we do, isn't it?" says Wolfington, stepping out of the shadows. He's dressed in a suit that is the same color as his shaggy, brown hair and wild beard. He leans against Alva's statue as if it's a castle pillar. "When we see someone making a mistake, it's in our nature to want to stop them. But sometimes we have to let them make their own choices."

"She's my sister. I'm supposed to protect her," I say desperately and look at the statue of Flora, waiting for her to come back to life and agree with me.

Wolfington nods. "You may want to, but like you, she's growing up and she's got to do it on her own."

"But she's doing it wrong," I say stubbornly, and he laughs.

"Mistakes are a part of life." He looks at Flora's statue. "When she's ready, she'll come around."

"And what if she doesn't?" I ask worriedly.

"Right now your only job is to find that goose." He pulls at his beard. "You're going to need all your strength and your wits in those woods. I lived in them for years, and you can get turned around in an instant. See things that aren't there. Some have even been fooled into believing things that are not true and embracing the worst version of themselves."

I shudder. The Hollow Woods sound worse than I thought. "Professor Harlow doesn't think we'll find anything."

"She could be right," he says truthfully. "But she also might be wrong. If that's the case, you're going to need the help of someone who knows how to navigate those woods. I know someone who does." I look up in surprise. "Our history is not a pleasant one, but if she gets the note I smuggled out, she'll do what's right and come find you. She's an excellent tracker, terrific marksman, and a true hunter. She's the best shot you've got." He hands me a small scroll.

I open the parchment and see coordinates to a spot right inside the Hollow Woods. "There's no name on here. How do I know who to look for?"

Wolfington smiles wolfishly. "My dear, I would have thought you'd already guessed. It's Little Red Riding Hood."

CHAPTER 15

Into the Woods

I feel like I've barely closed my eyes to get a good night's sleep before our trip when I'm yanked out of bed by the RS squad. They waste no time showing us the door.

"Headmaster Stiltskin forgot to mention one more thing," says Hansel as he tosses us out and throws our bags out behind us. "You've only got one week to complete your mission. Oh, and you're going to need new supplies for your journey. We took most of your loot out of your bags." He slams the door behind him, and I can hear him laughing.

"Creep!" Jocelyn yells as she stands dangerously close to the edge of the moat. Hungry crocodiles are snapping their jaws below. "We have one week? I can't even get a proper tracking spell up and running in a week! And now he took all our supplies! Cobbler, you should have been specific in your deal. You've doomed us to fail!"

"Jocelyn, don't be so witchy!" says Kayla. We all look at the moodiest fairy in the kingdom in surprise. "Let's gather our things, see what we still have, and make a plan. We can meet over by my family so I can say good-bye. I'm sure we can find a golden goose in seven days!" She grabs her bag and flies off ahead of us.

"I'm sorry, who was that?" asks Ollie, trudging off.

I grab my backpack and see something move in the front pocket. I lift it open. "Wilson! What are you doing in there?" The small mouse starts squeaking.

"He says he can help," says Hayley, misting herself all over.

I'm skeptical, but he did help us avoid getting sliced in two in the hallway, and he did find that magic bean. "Okay. I guess more help is always good." I stick him in my uniform pocket and feel him snuggle in. Then I walk over the moat and down the path to a cornfield where three unusually large trees stand looking out of place.

"Quack!" Peaches pops her head out of Maxine's bag as she trudges ahead of me. I growl.

"You said more help is good, and I couldn't leave her

behind," Maxine says. "With Flora not around, Stiltskin would probably...cook her for supper."

"Quack!" Peaches says in agreement, her voice being carried on the wind. The corn even has its own sound, whistling and creaking as the branches sway back and forth.

"We should only be so lucky," Jocelyn gripes as we reach Kayla and rest under the trees' shade. "That thing eats everything, and it never coughs up the same item!" She opens her bag. "Those RS squad creeps took all my potions. Good thing I hid some stuff in secret pockets."

"Me too," says Ollie. "Everyone dump your things, and let's see what we still have."

Between us, we have several cloaks, assorted small pocketknives, Jax's pocket watch, the broken glass slipper heel that Jocelyn gave me, a deck of cards, a small bag of fairy dust, a map of Enchantasia, and Maxine's mini magical scroll.

"They took all our food and water and most of our weapons," Jax says grimly. "All the wands we swiped from training class are gone too."

"We don't need a wand when we have me," says Jocelyn, producing a purple fireball. "I also swiped candy. It will be perfect to use on hungry giants, and Harlow says there are loads of them in those woods." We all stare warily at the dark forest.

"They're not that big," says Jax nervously. "I hear they're only half as tall as the giants from the land of magic beans."

"We're going to need more than candy to survive that place," I say worriedly.

"Good thing we're here to help," says Rapunzel, stepping out from behind a nearby cornstalk with Princess Ella and Flora's daughters, Dahlia and Azalea. The four are almost unrecognizable in pale-yellow and green cloaks that blend in with the corn.

Dahlia rushes toward me. Her face is tear streaked. "I know she was trying to protect us, but she was foolish to make that deal." Azalea blows her nose loudly. "You have to save Mother."

"I wish my stepmother had come to me first." Ella removes her hood to reveal a silver tiara and her white-blond hair. "No matter our differences, I always thought this school was a splendid idea, and I won't see it fall into Rumpelstiltskin's hands." She looks at Rapunzel. "If we have to, we'll take it back by force."

"You're going to attack the school?" I ask, my mind immediately going to Anna. "With all the kids in it?"

"If it comes to that," Rapunzel says gravely. "We'll protect the students the best we can, but we can't let a power-hungry troll like him brainwash a school of semi-villains and thieves."

"It won't come to that," Jax insists. "We will find that goose."

"You have a week to try to find the goose, but if you don't return by then, we will have to proceed with our own plan," Princess Ella tells us.

We're all silent. I feel like the clock is already ticking.

Kayla leans against the tallest tree. "We will find the goose! Mother and my sisters will send their fairy army to guide us to her in the woods."

Rapunzel and I look at each other. "That's well and good, but we brought food, water, and some tools to help you too." She drops a small, gray bag at our feet.

"No offense, Princess, but I doubt that bag can hold more than a can of soup," says Jocelyn.

Ella smiles serenely. "Tap the bag strap with your foot." Jocelyn skeptically does what she's told. Within seconds, the bag begins to inflate into the shape of a miniature house.

"It's a pop-up castle," says Rapunzel, and Maxine, Kayla,

and Ollie ooh. "At full size, there are chambers for you all to sleep in, a pantry stocked with food, and some maps."

"Gingerbread, that's cool!" Ollie says. "I wonder if they make a pop-up pirate ship version."

"I hope it has separate sleeping chambers," Jocelyn sniffs. "I like my space."

Ella taps the bottom-right corner of the castle with her heel, and it deflates to regular bag size.

I pick up the bag and throw it over my shoulder. "This will help us a lot."

"Our royal guards have spent time in the Hollow Woods," Ella says. "You can get turned around very easily." She points to a small lake in the distance near the edge of the woods. "Follow the water. It cuts straight through the forest. We also brought this, but only use it if you absolutely need it." She pulls a rolled-up mat out of her cloak and hands it to Jax. The rug pops open, and a fringed edge tickles Jax's chin.

"Blue!" he exclaims. "What are you doing here?" He pats the rug, and it shakes and shimmies like Jax's and Ollie's fairy pets that we left in Harlow's care. I hope she remembers to feed them.

"We took him from Pete," says Rapunzel. "Snow told him Blue owed the royals after helping to destroy our party." The rug sails over our heads. "When we told him what you were up against, he was more than happy to come along."

"But remember, magic does not work the same way in the woods," Rapunzel reminds us. "Don't trick yourselves into thinking Blue can fly you out of any precarious situation, like getting sucked into a giant's mouth."

Maxine gulps.

"I'm sure that won't happen," Ella adds hastily. "We wish you all the best of luck. We're counting on you." Ella smiles before turning back into the cornfield with the others. "If anyone can find that goose, it is you Fairy Tale Reform School students."

In the distance, I hear a wolf howl and pray it's a regular wolf. Not the Big Bad Wolf kind. Jocelyn studies the map. "I say we go this way." She points to a clearing down the hill that leads to a gap in the tree line along the edge of the forest. Even though it's only midday, the shadow the forest casts is almost pitch-black.

"I don't know." I hesitate. "A clearing like that looks like a trap."

"Oh, Cobbler," Jocelyn tsks. "You think you know everything! The clearing leads us right past the stream we are supposed to follow. This is the best way in."

Jax and Ollie read over our shoulders. "I say we try it," Jax agrees.

Hayley mists herself again. "Yeah. Wilson and Peaches don't seem to be sending up any red flags, and animals can sense danger."

I feel uneasy. My gut is telling me to go another way. We have to reach those coordinates to meet Little Red Riding Hood before nightfall. I unroll the piece of paper in my pocket. "Before we go, there's something I have to tell you guys."

"Later!" says Kayla, flying ahead with Blue. The others run after her.

"Wait!" I trail behind them, trying to get their attention. I hear a whistling sound and tell myself it's just the wind. "I have coordinates Wolfington gave me. He asked someone to meet us."

"Who? A wolf?" Ollie jokes. The others laugh.

I purse my lips. They'll never believe me if I tell them. I just need them to see her.

"I'll tell you when we get there." Jax frowns. I'm not helping, I can tell.

"Secrets already?" Jocelyn rolls her eyes. "This is not how you start a quest!"

We all start bickering, and it's impossible to hear who is saying what. Without even realizing it, we've passed the clearing and entered the forest. I blink to get used to the darkness. I can see Maxine's eyeball rolling wildly as we look around. There are lots of trees, rocks, some small creatures scurrying about, and a stream flowing along our path. Maybe the Hollow Woods are just woods after all.

"See?" Jocelyn says, turning to face us with her hands on her hips. "I told you this was the perfect way in. And look around." She walks backward for a second. "We're—"

Jocelyn doesn't get to finish her sentence. I feel something wind around my feet before I even know what's happening. A clump of branches pulls up around us, forming a net. It goes flying into the air and ties itself shut high in the trees. We're trapped.

CHAPTER 16

Red-y for Anything

"Cobbler, get your knee off my chin!" Jocelyn huffs as she dislodges her arm from behind Ollie's head.

We're piled on top of one another like an overstuffed sandwich, and we're hanging high in the air. People are bound to be testy.

"I will if someone will get their boot off my butt!" I push Jax's boot out of my face. "This one is on you."

"Me!" Jocelyn cries. "You wouldn't tell us who you wanted to meet with!" We start to argue, and Jax whistles.

"Can we continue this fight on the ground?" he asks. "If I can reach my pocket watch, I might be able to blast open a piece of the netting."

"No!" we all cry.

"We'll fall to our deaths," Kayla says as our net swings precariously. "Who knows how much weight this net was meant to hold?"

I roll to one side, pushing Hayley's hair out of my face, and look down. *Whoa.* The trees in Hollow Woods are almost as tall as the Fairy Tale Reform School castle, which I can just see the top of from here. I also have a pretty good view of the woods, which go on for miles. How are we going to find a golden goose in this place? In the distance, I watch a group of trees sway, and it's not even windy. "Guys," I say nervously. "Some of the trees are moving. A lot."

"Must be giants," Maxine says. "They use nets like these to catch their dinner."

"Blast the hole," Ollie says hurriedly. "We'll take our chances! I don't want to be someone's dinner! I'm sure Kayla can fly us all to safety."

Kayla frowns. "I can't even open my wings in this mess."

We hear a low roar followed by heavy footsteps that make the ground shake.

"Great," Hayley says. "We've taken two steps, and we're already done for."

Swish! I hear something fly past the net and hit a mark

above our heads. An arrow has pierced the branch our net is dangling from, and a long rope hangs from it to the ground.

"Move to one side!" someone yells up, and we all lean to the right. A second arrow narrowly misses Ollie's arm as it slices a hole in the net. Nice aim. I hear a whistle and look down. I see a darkened figure in a brown hood and cape. "Make that hole wider, then climb out and use the rope to climb down. Go one at a time, and you'll be fine."

Kayla looks worried. "I don't know… Do we trust this person with our—"

"*ROAR!*" The trees around us begin to sway as the footsteps grow louder and louder.

"Never mind. Let's go." Kayla climbs to the hole and flies out.

"Me next!" Hayley says. She mists her face, then climbs out, and we watch her shimmy down. Jocelyn and Ollie are next. They both make it down without a problem.

"You first, thief," Jax says.

"No, you first," I say stubbornly.

"Ladies always go first," Jax insists.

"That's so royal." I roll my eyes. "I am not going first on principle!"

"*ROAR!*"

Our tree begins to sway, and I see the giant's face come into view. His skin is pasty white, and his face is deformed with eyes that are as dark as coal. He's wearing a one-shouldered animal-skin romper that barely covers all the dirt on his body.

"On second thought, let's both go." I reach for the rope. Jax is right behind me. As we climb out, I hear Kayla.

"Look out!" she shouts.

I look up and see the giant's hand reach for the net. Our rope begins to sway. *Swish!* An arrow pierces his meaty hand, and he lets out a loud scream. His rancid breath blows on us. Gross. Can't stop now. We start to descend.

"Faster, thief!" Jax says as we shimmy down, but we're not fast enough. The giant's hand takes another swipe at the rope.

I feel his fingers brush my hair.

"Jump!" Jax says when we're still several feet off the ground.

I don't argue. I let go of the rope and feel myself rush to the ground. *Whoosh!* We land on a pile of leaves at the others' feet, and the ground shakes. The giant is still coming for us. He steps shakily forward, and we all scream. The person in the cape steps over us, taking aim with her bow and arrow. She hits the giant squarely between the eyes, and he lets out a fierce roar.

"Gotcha," the figure says before removing her cloak. We all gasp.

It's Little Red Riding Hood, except she's not so little anymore. Her skin is as bronze as the body armor she is wearing under her cape. It protects her chest, her elbows, and even her thighs, covering the simple beige shirt and brown, tight pantaloons she has on. She points to my feet and grins.

"Nice boots," says Red. I notice hers are identical to my own.

The giant roars again, and we all freeze. Red is the only one who is calm.

"That beast just won't stop," she says with a sly smile. "Looks like I'll have to teach him a lesson." He roars again. "You guys should go."

Ollie and Kayla cling to Red's arm. "We want to stay with you," Ollie says, and Kayla nods. The ground shakes as the giant begins to move again.

"You won't last ten minutes in this fight," Red tells them. She looks at Jax and me. "Make your way to the Emerald Coast Cliffs. They're in the center of the forest, but they're obscured by trees and dense foliage. You'll find your goose there."

"How did you...?" Ollie starts to say as Red reloads her bow with a strange-looking arrow that is smoking.

"I'll come find you when the coast is clear." Red's arrow flies through the air and hits the giant in the chest. Smoke billows out of the arrow, clouding the giant's vision. She holds out the bow and arrows to me. "Take this. It may come in handy if you come across wolves."

"Wolves?" Maxine, Kayla, and Ollie repeat.

"I don't know how to use it," I say quickly. Another roar makes the ground shake more violently.

"Then you'll have to learn." Red pulls a spare bow-and-arrow set out of some nearby brush. "When you get to the cliff, make your way down. I'll be at the bottom." The ground shakes again. "Now go!" Red takes off toward the giant and fires another arrow. We watch as he stumbles sideways. The tree we were just hanging from begins to crack and fall in our direction.

We don't stick around. We dodge and weave past falling limbs as we head in the direction she told us to go. After a while, it feels like we're running for hours, jumping through muddy puddles and over rocks, and crossing a huge chasm on a swaying rope bridge, but still there's no sign of a cliff.

"We have to be going the wrong way," Jocelyn says, lighting the path with a purple orb. "It's so dark in here I can barely see my hand."

I shudder. It feels like the trees are closing in on us. When I glance up at the sky, the sun is barely visible over treetops that twist and wind together like a net.

"The cliff has to be here somewhere," Jax says. "Come on, goosie, where are you?"

"*Goosie?*" I can't help but giggle.

"Goose," Jax corrects himself sheepishly. "The golden goose is a legend Aesop himself used to tell. Some versions of the story say the goose was killed for riches that never came. Others say she's hidden somewhere safe where her treasured golden feathers can't be plucked. No one knows which version of the story is true."

"Great," I grumble and hear a low howl in the distance. I put my hand on the bow and hope I am just hearing things.

Hayley stops short. "Did anyone hear that?" she whispers.

Several wolves howl in unison.

"There is more than one," Hayley says, and none of us question her. After all, she can talk to animals. "And they're not friendly. We need to get out of here."

"Look! There is a clearing up ahead." Kayla flies off, then comes back a minute later. "It's the cliffs! I can see geese in the water down there. The golden goose has to be there. We just have to get to the bottom."

"If the golden goose is down there, getting to the bottom won't be easy," Jocelyn says grimly. "I'm sure there is some sort of test."

We hear another giant roar. The howling is getting louder—and closer too. Behind us, the trees begin to sway again.

"Come on!" Kayla says.

I hold the bow ready in case a wolf or a giant gets close, but I can barely run and ready an arrow at the same time. How does Red do it?

As we get closer, the dark trees give way to a brighter light. We burst into the rocky clearing, and I feel like I'm seeing a mirage. In the middle of the dense forest is a magnificent lake far below. Waterfalls trickle down the rocky ledge to the shimmering lake. Peaches quacks loudly. Wilson pokes his head out of my pocket, sees the cliff, then burrows back inside. Some help he is.

"There has to be a way down," Maxine says. "'What are we supposed to do, fly?"

Jax pulls the rug out of his pack and shakes it open. Blue straightens like an arrow and spins around us. "We can now."

"That will only hold two of us," Jocelyn reminds him. "Kayla can fly down, but flight can't be the only way. Not everyone travels with a magic carpet or a fairy."

"Plus, the princesses said the rug might not even work in the forest," Jocelyn says. "And for once, I agree with them."

"Mermaids aren't big on flying either," Hayley says. "There has to be another option." She looks over the edge. "That's quite the jump."

"We have to give Blue a shot," Jax insists.

We hear a loud roar. The giant is back. Does that mean he got Red? I don't want to even think about being alone in the forest right now. I hold the bow and arrow and prepare to shoot. The arrow falls out of the bow and hits the ground.

Jocelyn laughs. She lights a purple fireball. "I'll hang back with Cobbler while you take the first trip. Her arrows can't even hit a rock."

"We have to get a move on," Jax says. Kayla lifts into the air. Jax helps Ollie onto the rug. Jocelyn, Maxine, and I stand ready for the approaching wolves and giant, while the other group heads toward the chasm. Jax, Ollie, and

Blue barely reach the edge of the cliff when *bam!* They get thrown backward. Ollie and Jax roll off the rug and land at our feet.

I run over. "Are you okay?" I help them up.

"Told you there'd be a protection charm," Jocelyn says smugly. "No one can fly over that lake unless..." She begins walking around the ledge. Without warning, she steps off the cliff. Maxine screams. "Look!" Jocelyn's balance is shaky as she stands inches from the cliff edge, seemingly in midair. We rush over and look. "It's a step. I bet this is an invisible staircase."

"*Or* you're about to walk the plank to your death," Ollie says.

"*Or* this is a test and Jocelyn is right," I realize.

Maxine perks up. "You're right! Every quest has tests. Maybe this is our first one."

"If it is, and those wolves and giant are after us, they won't be able to follow," Jocelyn guesses. "I hope." A chorus of howls answers us.

"Guys," Hayley says warily. "They're almost here!"

"*ROAR!*" The trees behind us begin to fall and crash to the ground as the giant makes his way into the clearing. In the light, he's even taller and more fearsome looking than

I imagined. His misshapen eyes glance down at us, and he takes a step forward.

I'm shaking, but I aim an arrow at his arm that is outstretched toward us. Jocelyn appears at my side with a fireball.

"Together!" she shouts. "Now!"

Her fireball shoots into the air at the same time my arrow does. They make contact with the giant's arm, and he stumbles back in pain.

"That won't hold him long," I say as I hear the wolves approaching the clearing. "We need to try those steps."

"We might fall!" Maxine cries.

The wolves burst through the trees. We're out of time. "We don't have a choice," Jax says. "Go!"

Jocelyn reaches the edge first and steps forward again. We all inhale sharply, and I shut my eyes. When I open them, Jocelyn is seemingly floating in midair. She takes another step, and we see her drop ever so slightly. Kayla gasps.

"I'm fine!" Jocelyn shouts. "The steps are going down—*Gilly!*"

I turn around. The wolves are charging toward us, along with the giant.

"Everyone go!" I pull another arrow out of the quiver as the others rush by me. Jocelyn tries to aim a fireball, but now that she's on the staircase, the magic disintegrates in the air. I shoot an arrow at a wolf and miss. The giant comes running my way, and the ground shakes so much that I fall to the ground.

"Gilly!" Kayla cries.

I turn around. Everyone has reached the steps but me. The wolves are almost at the edge. If Jocelyn is right and I leap onto a step, they won't be able to follow. I just need a few more seconds to get back up. From the ground, I pull another arrow out of the quiver. As the giant's hand brushes my arm, I aim at his thigh and fire. He howls in pain and stumbles backward, sending the wolves running in opposite directions.

I have my chance and I take it. I quickly stand up and leap, trying not to think about what will happen if I miss.

My feet hit the invisible ground. I'm suspended in midair, sky above and water far, far below me. The others are already walking down. I'm alive. I look back at the cliff. The giant and the wolves have vanished.

I can't help but smile. *Take that, Stiltskin.*

We're one step closer to finding your golden goose.

CHAPTER 17

A-Questing We Will Go

When we finally reach the bottom of the phantom staircase, Red is somehow already there, standing on the rocky shoreline along the blue-green lake. The water is so bright that it almost looks magical. Maybe it is.

"Took you long enough," Red says as we all collapse on the sand.

"How did you beat us down here?" I ask, out of breath. "We thought the giant got you."

"Me?" Red laughs. "Never. Besides, he wasn't after me. He was after you. This is your quest, and many would like to see you fail."

Kayla tries to sit up—and fails. "How do you know about the quest?"

"Wolfington told me, of, course," Red says. "You're trying to find the goose with the golden egg, right? That's why I said to meet me at the Emerald Cove Cliffs. If that goose exists, she'd be near water, and this is the only large body I've ever found in the Hollow Woods."

"You're seriously friends with a wolf who tried to eat you?" Ollie asks.

Red examines an arrow in her quiver. "We may not be the best of friends, but we understand each other. I did get away, as you might remember."

"But you don't want revenge for what he did to you and Granny?" Jocelyn asks.

"Why would I want revenge?" Red asks. "Whatever demons Wolfington has to face every full moon are more than enough punishment. Besides, if he hadn't tried to take me out, I never would have found out how fearless I can be." She smiles. "I am one of the few hunters who dares to take on the Hollow Woods. Wolfington taught me that I will never allow myself to be someone's prey again."

I'm speechless. Fighting Wolfington helped Red figure out who she was?

"If you're really the Red we've heard so much about, why

aren't you wearing a red cape?" Hayley asks and looks at the rest of us. "What if this is just another one of Stiltskin's tricks? How do we know we can trust her?"

I hadn't even thought of that. We quickly sit up.

Red flips the interior of her cape out so we can see; it's deep red. "It's an update. This way no one can ever see me coming," she says. "The version I sell in the village is the classic bright red." She looks at me. "At least it was the version I sold before your sister blew up my shop."

Fiddlesticks. "You know who I am?" I ask.

"I know a lot about you, Gillian Cobbler," she says, looking directly at me with her light-brown eyes. "Wolfington thinks you have what it takes to take on an impossible mission, but I'm not sure I trust someone who would foolishly make a deal with Rumpelstiltskin."

"It was a deal I couldn't refuse," I say. "If we find the goose and bring it back to him, he'll give control of our school back to the Wicked Stepmother. He'll free my friend Kayla's family and some students who don't belong in FTRS." *Like Anna.* "Will you help us find it?"

She sighs. "I got you this far, but I don't know. Stiltskin doesn't make deals people can keep. Others have tried and failed. Many older and wiser than you." She eyes us all skeptically. "So why should I work with a bunch of kids, especially a young pickpocket?"

I think for a second, choosing my words carefully so there is no mistaking them. When I look at Red again, my eyes feel like they're on fire. "We may be kids, but we're stronger than we look. We've fought Alva twice and handled the Evil Queen. Stiltskin needs that goose, and we don't plan on going home 'til we get the job done." The others nod.

Red smiles. "Good answer. I'm in." She leans against one of the rocks on the beach. "It still won't be easy. Legend has it that you have to pass three tests to get near that goose: one to prove your strength, one to prove your courage, and one to prove intelligence. If she's really down here, you've already handled courage—jumping off a cliff, not knowing what was below. But the other two—strength and brains—will be much tougher. Let's rest here for a bit and regroup. We're safe for now."

"No argument from me." Ollie pulls out the pop-up castle. "Who wants goulash for lunch? I'll cook."

Peaches quacks madly. Maxine hands her a biscuit and says, "Why don't you swim around and see if you can get the other geese to tell you if the golden goose is near here and where we can find her?" Peaches quacks again, then waddles into the water.

"I'll check the golden goose stories for clues," Kayla says.

"Cobbler, you should stay here with me," Red says. "You need to work on your shot. You've got terrible aim."

"Thanks." My face feels hot.

"You're not a total lost cause," Red adds. "You did track your way to the clearing, held off the giant—barely—escaped a pack of wolves, and bravely waited 'til you were the last one left to step onto the staircase. You've got guts."

"How did you see all that?" Jax asks.

"I see everything," Red says and looks at me again. "And I'm surprised this one just wants to be a shoemaker."

My skin prickles. "Only because that's the way it works in Enchantasia," I snap. "You are what your parents are. He's a royal, she's the sister of the former evil queen, and I'm a shoemaker's daughter."

Red pulls a bright-red apple out of her sack and begins to peel it with a pocketknife. She slices the apple and hands a piece to each of us. "Interesting. I didn't peg you for the type that settles."

"I don't have a choice!"

Suddenly I hear myself: I sound like Anna. So this is how it feels to be trapped. Anna wants this life and thinks she can't have it, and—I'm finally realizing—I don't want it. And there's nothing I can do about it.

"There's nothing wrong with being a shoemaker if that's what your goal in life is," Red says. "Royals and evil queens tend to be able to carve out their own destinies, and a shoemaker has a clear path. I guess you just need to ask yourself: Is that the path you want to be on?" I am quiet. "If it's not, what do you want to change about yourself, Gilly Cobbler?" She pulls herself up on the rock and lies down in the sun. "At least, that's the question I would ask myself if this were my quest. Quests are a perfect time to figure out who you are."

I storm off and head to the water.

"You okay?" Jax asks after he follows me there.

"Who does Red think she is?" I grumble. "She has no idea what I'm capable of."

"She doesn't," Jax agrees. "But do you?" I look at him strangely. "I'm just asking because you don't seem happy with trade school. Every time you talk about it, you get a look. I know that look because it's the same way I feel about Royal Academy." He stares at the water, and a school of geese floats by. None of them are golden. "I don't mind being on a *Royally Yours* poster if there is more to my story than just my face and title. I have to figure out what that story is." He knocks my shoulder. "Maybe you do too. Red can't decide it for you."

I smile a little. Red is a huntress and a fighter. Not a girl who cried wolf. Anna wants to be more than a shoemaker's apprentice. Maybe I can be more than I think I am too. "Maybe you're right."

"Guys!" Ollie pops out of the castle carrying a green leather book that has a picture of the mythical goose on the cover. "'Listen to what we just read in this book! It says, 'What treasures are buried in your imagination? Search below for the key and unlock the castle. Then the golden answers you seek will be yours.'" He taps a picture inside the book with his dirty fingernails.

"See this? The goose is sitting on an island in the middle of the lake. On the island is a small castle, but it sort of looks like a rock, just like that rock out there." He points to the middle of the lake, and I blink hard in the bright light. It's small, but there is definitely an island out there. The more I look at its ragged edges, the more it begins to look like a miniature castle too. Could our goose be hiding inside?

"You think this nursery rhyme is the real deal?" Jax asks.

"It's the only lead we have," Jocelyn says. "But I'm not sure what to do about the key. It could be anywhere."

I hear honking and look up. Peaches, the lone ugly duckling in a sea of white swans, is honking her head off. Maxine comes out of the castle when she hears her.

"Peaches? Come back here!" Maxine calls as the duck starts pecking at the geese. One dips its head under the water and comes back up with a fish. Peaches swipes it from him and swims quickly back to shore. "Peaches! That's not nice!" Maxine scolds as the duck waddles up to us and swallows the fish. Two seconds later, the fish comes back up as a piece of blue coral. Peaches quacks again.

"I think Peaches is trying to tell us the key is underwater," Hayley says. "If it is, I can swim down and find it."

"This is easy!" Kayla claps. "Mother?" she yells to the sky. "We'll be back soon!"

"Red, what do you think?" I ask worriedly.

"Don't look at me," Red says. "I can get you places, but

this is your quest. You have to make the hard choices. If you think she can find the key, then let her."

I don't like that answer. I feel even more worrisome when Hayley removes her shoes and wades into the water. Her body begins to shimmer to a pearl color, then she disappears below the surface. When she comes back up a minute later, her legs have been replaced with a shiny tail.

"Wait!" I yell, and everyone looks at me. Red watches closely. "Something isn't right. The strength quest can't be that simple."

"It's only easy because we have a mermaid with us," Jocelyn says.

"Having a mermaid on our quest is a happy accident, not a sign of strength," I say. "I think if that key is down there, it will take more than just Hayley to get it. What if we only get one shot to grab the key? We don't want to blow it." Red grins. "I think the strongest have to go down and help her."

"How are we going to last underwater?" Jocelyn asks.

"Same as before." I pick up the coral that Peaches gave us. "Didn't you place something like this over our noses and mouths so we could swim in Cleo's tank?"

"Yes," Hayley says. "They're coral hearts. You can breathe

underwater for at least fifteen minutes with them, maybe more, but you can only use one each. I'll grab some." Hayley is back in less than a minute with the bright-blue coral.

"Who's up for a swim?" Ollie asks. "I may be small, but I'm an excellent swimmer because of all my time on the high seas."

"I'll go too," says Jax and shows his biceps. "*Royally Yours* says I have the best biceps in the kingdom." We all groan.

I look at the others. Maxine will sink like a rock. Fairies are not the best swimmers either. "I'll go," I say.

Jocelyn immediately gets fired up. "Why not me?"

I hug her, which I know looks odd, and whisper in her ear, "Because if I don't make it back, you're the strongest shot we've got at making it out of here with that goose." We look at one another.

"Fine, but don't die on me," Jocelyn says. "I don't want the headache of going the rest of the way alone." I don't let her see me smile. "Gilly can go!" she calls to the others.

Hayley hands Jax, Ollie, and me each a coral heart. We wade into warm water up to our shoulders. I look back at the others on the shoreline, then place the blue coral over my lips and nose and plunge underwater. The coral heart knows exactly what to do. I can feel the oxygen filling my lungs, and I can breathe normally.

Amazing! I look around. Last time I was under the sea, I was too panicked to enjoy the view, but now… *Wow.* The Little Mermaid is one lucky, uh, mermaid.

Hayley beckons for us to follow so we swim farther into the lake, looking at the reeds all around us. After a little while, Hayley stops at a large rock, and I realize it's the island. The four of us swim around it looking for clues.

The rock feels like ice and is smooth to the touch, but I don't see any markings or keys dangling anywhere. I feel Ollie tap me and point to the reeds below our feet. When the reeds sway, I notice something further down—a gold table at the bottom of the sea with a top as clear as glass. We all look at each other. Why would a table be down here?

The key has to be on it.

Hayley moves to swim closer, but I notice her struggling against the current. The closer we get to the table, the harder the sea grass is to swim through. Jax and Ollie try to cut it with their small knives, but they can barely break off a tiny reed. We slowly fight our way through, wasting air, but we eventually make it to the benches on either side of the table.

I'm sure we're running out of time. Quickly, we run our hands along the glass and down the legs of the table but find nothing. It has to be here! I know it. Next, I run my hands along the clear underside of the table, and that's when I feel something hard. It doesn't look like anything is there, but when I duck below the table, I spot the clear box. I pull on it, but it won't open so I motion to Jax for his knife. I pound away, trying to crack the box.

Suddenly, the reeds around the table stop moving. The small fish that were just floating by my hands zip away and vanish. Something's wrong. Hayley's eyes widen and she motions for us to leave, but I know the key is in that box. Ignoring Hayley's frantic arm movements, I hit the box again and this time a gold key drops into my hands. I hold it up excitedly, but Hayley doesn't look happy. She's practically frantic, her tail swinging back and forth madly. That's when I hear a high-pitched squeal and a crackling sound, and my smile vanishes as I see what's coming for us.

A massive red electric eel is rocketing through the water toward us, his skin flashing like lightning. His tail brushes a tall reed, and it disintegrates. His eyes lock on the key.

Hayley doesn't need words to tell me what I already know: swim for your life!

She grabs me and Jax, who grabs Ollie as the eel comes crashing into the table and the whole thing evaporates into dust. We make for the reeds but can barely break through them to hide. The grass seems to be pushing us backward into the eel's path! Lightning flashes dangerously close as Jax tries to knife his way through the reeds. Ollie and Hayley use their teeth. I clutch the key tightly, fearing it will fall into the dark reeds below. We're goners.

Then from above I see a flash of purple light. Orbs begin rocketing into the water, and the reeds suddenly part and curl away from the flame. An orb hits the eel, and it screeches angrily. Hayley doesn't hesitate. She grabs our hands and shoots toward the surface at such speed that I feel my coral heart get sucked from my lips. When we hit the surface, I realize we're still a way from shore.

"*Move!*" Jocelyn screams. She continues to shoot fireball after fireball at the moving, red target that has produced the lake's sudden waves.

The eel is moving so fast that I fear it will devour us whole, but Hayley zips us through the water, pulling us like a train. She's only inches ahead of the eel. I want to scream, but no sound escapes me 'til Hayley hits the shoreline and we race onto the beach.

Just like that, the eel vanishes. The lake returns to calm. The geese fly back to the water as if nothing's happened. But something has.

I hold up the key, still clutched firmly in my hand. Everyone cheers, and the rest of us collapse on the shore.

"I'll tell you one thing," Ollie says as he takes gulps of air. "We are not swimming back out to that island. Next time, we fly."

CHAPTER 18

The Final Quest

Red kicks my wet boots. "Get up," she says, standing at the ready with a bow and arrow.

Geez. Why's she being so bossy? She didn't have to fight that thing. "I…just…need…five…minutes," I say, taking deep breaths.

"Me too." Hayley sits up slowly and shakes out her legs. I watch her skin go from almost translucent white back to an almost bronze color. "I've been in the water half my life and never seen anything like it."

"Up! You passed two quests. The universe won't like that. I bet you don't have five minutes 'til the next one starts." Red nocks an arrow into the bow.

"Listen, Red, she just fought off an eel," Jocelyn says as

she tears through a spell book with Kayla. "I highly doubt something else is going to jump out at us while we're sitting on the beach. We need time to figure out how to get back out to the island with the key. We obviously can't swim, and I assume there are magical protection charms that keep us from flying, like back on the cliff."

Ollie sits up. "I am not going back in that water, and if something else is coming for us, I want to make it to that island first. Let's give Blue a shot." He whistles to the magic carpet. It races to his side and wiggles like a dog. "What's the worst that can happen?" He slowly climbs onto the carpet.

"I'll go with you." Kayla flies on and sits beside him. "If something goes wrong, hopefully I can carry you away since you're small."

"Who are you calling small?" Ollie asks as Blue takes off like a shot. I watch in amazement as they easily zoom to the island and hover next to it. We all cheer.

"Quiet," Red hisses. She looks around the shoreline suspiciously. The water is calm. The geese are quiet. The only thing out of the ordinary seems to be us. What's she so worried about? Red drops my bow and arrow on me. She doesn't take her eye off the rocky cliff. "Up. Now. Load your weapon!"

"What's—" My words get caught in my throat when I hear the snarling. I look up and see a blur of brown fur race down the mountain. It's moving faster than any carpet I've flown, quicker than any Pegasus or even that eel. Whatever it is, it's headed straight toward us. Red begins firing arrows.

I motion to Maxine. "Toss me one of your necklaces."

Maxine clutches her neck. "Why?"

"I need it to hold the key. Quick!" Maxine tosses me a chain, and I slip the key onto it, then put it around my neck for safekeeping. The snarling intensifies as I fumble with my bow. My quiver of arrows falls on the ground as Red fires again and again.

"Cobbler, help me!" Red yells.

"I'm trying!" I scramble to pick up all my arrows. I look up. The blur is getting closer.

"Don't panic!" Ollie shouts. "We'll send Blue back, and you can come over." Kayla goes to dismount, and an electric shock sends her scrambling back onto the carpet. They try to bring Blue back to shore, but it won't budge. "We're stuck!"

"Plan B! Everyone into the water," Hayley shouts. She dips a toe into the water and gets thrown backward.

"Great! New protection charms!" Jocelyn complains. "Something wants us stuck right here in this creature's path."

I fire at the thing and miss.

Jocelyn readies her fireballs. "I'll stop it." She conjures fireball after fireball, but each blast barely reaches the mountain before fizzling out. "For the love of Grimm, something is messing with my magic!"

"Don't you see?" Red keeps her eye on the moving target. "If your third quest is brains, magic won't help you. You have to outsmart this thing!"

The beast stops moving and lets out a menacing howl that I can feel in my bones.

"It's a wolf!" Maxine says. "Red, you know how to beat those!"

"That's no wolf," Red says as we watch the thing pace on a ledge a few feet above us.

I can see it clearly from here. It's about fifteen feet up. It's longer than a wolf and bigger with long legs; shaggy, brown fur; a long neck; and a black snout. It has sharp rows of teeth that make me feel like I might pass out. I hold my bow shakily.

Jax appears at my side with a sword raised high. "That's a bandersnatch."

"Can't be! They're a myth," Jocelyn says. It's the first time I've ever seen her nervous.

"Like the golden goose?" Jax asks.

"Stop debating whether it's real or not! It's almost here!" Red shouts as the beast jumps from a low ledge and rushes down the beach. It's only ten feet away now. We start to run in the opposite direction.

My mind is in a total panic. How do you outsmart a mythical creature that could swallow you in one gulp?

We reach the other end of the beach and find ourselves beside a rock wall leading up to the cliff we came down from. We've got nowhere to go. Jax tries to give me a foothold to climb up, but I keep slipping down. Ollie and Kayla are shouting something I can't hear, and Peaches is quacking madly. I'm momentarily distracted. I watch the duck reach into Maxine's bag and pull out a bright-red cape.

"Aren't your new capes supposed to protect the wearer from harm?" Maxine asks.

"Those capes are just for show," Red says as she fires arrow after arrow, but they do nothing to slow the beast down. At a loss for what else to do, I join Red and do the same.

"I thought I was good at tricks," Jocelyn says as she flings fireballs that fizzle out.

Instead of trying to get away like the rest of us, Peaches waddles toward the bandersnatch. Suddenly, Wilson sticks his head out of my pocket, climbs down my arm, then jumps onto the sand and follows her.

"Peaches!" Maxine cries. She tries to go after the duck, but we hold her back.

"Wilson!" I yell. "What are you doing? You want to be its lunch?"

The bandersnatch is closing in. I can see its dark, beady eyes and its mangy fur. Saliva drips out of its mouth as it snarls and gnashes its teeth. Peaches and Wilson head straight toward it. The bandersnatch stops right in front of them and sizes them up for its next meal.

"How could you sell fake capes?" Maxine cries. "I thought this could help us!"

"Sometimes it doesn't matter if something is real. You just have to believe it is," Red shouts.

"That's it," I realize as the bandersnatch paces in front of Peaches and Wilson and does nothing. "We can't show it we're afraid. It hasn't eaten those two yet because they're not scared. If we can show we're fearless, it will let us pass."

The bandersnatch bares its teeth again, but Peaches holds firm.

I'm right. I have to be. Because if I'm wrong...

I take a step forward and Maxine gasps. Then I take another. Jocelyn and Jax fall in line beside me, and finally Hayley and Maxine join too. I can feel everyone shaking as we approach the beast. The bandersnatch eyes us curiously as it continues to growls menacingly. I stop next to Peaches and Wilson and try to control my breathing. The beast circles me, sniffing. Its breath is rancid and its snout is dangerously close to my throat, but I use all my willpower to keep from freaking out. On either side of me, I feel my friends do the same.

"Stay very still," I whisper under my breath as the bandersnatch continues to growl. I wish I could close my eyes and will this moment to be over.

Jocelyn takes my hand, I take Jax's, and we all form a chain. Peaches and Wilson slip between our feet. The bandersnatch growls again, and I try not to flinch as it paces down the row. It howls one more time, then runs down the beach, leaving a trail of dust behind.

I can't believe it.

"It worked," Jax says. We jump up and down.

Hayley hits me in the shoulder. "Look!"

A bridge has formed from the shore to the island. I see Ollie and Kayla finally hop off Blue and set foot on the shoreline.

Kayla motions to us. "Come on!"

I look at the others.

This is really happening. We've survived a bandersnatch, giants, sea creatures, and an impossible fall down a cliff face. That goose is ours.

CHAPTER 19

Decision Time

Once we've safely crossed the bridge over the lake to the small island, I finally remove the key from around my neck. Red is waiting back on the shore just in case something goes wrong and we need an escape plan. Everyone starts examining the rocks to find a keyhole. Up close, the rocks' jagged edges really do make it look like a small castle, just like the one in the picture book.

"Keyhole spotted!" Ollie points to a small opening etched in the rocky stone. "We pirates can spot buried treasure from a mile away." We push moss away from the keyhole, and I place the key in the lock. Miraculously, it clicks and unlocks without any monsters showing up. Whew.

Maxine puts a hand on my arm as I go to push the rock

door open. "What if the golden goose is in there and it won't come back with us?"

"Then we kidnap it," Jocelyn says simply, and everyone looks at her. "This is our goal—get the goose, turn it over to Stiltskin, and get our lives and family back. We come first."

Maxine bites her large lip. "But the golden goose is one of a kind, which is why it's so protected. Do we really want to hand it over to the evilest man we know?"

Peaches quacks in earnest. Maybe she knows something we don't. Like this bridge is going to evaporate in five minutes and we'll be stranded here.

"We're doing it for the greater good," I say, trying to sound sure of myself. "Kayla will get her family back, we get Flora again, and FTRS is free of Stiltskin. Stealing one goose is a small price to pay." Everyone else nods, but Maxine doesn't answer me.

"Let's see if we've found our goose." I take a deep breath, and Jax and I push on the heavy door.

"Whoa," Ollie says breathlessly. "I was not expecting this."

My thoughts exactly. While the outside of this rocky castle looks incredibly small, the inside is magically one hundred times that size! Waterfalls, caverns, and even a blazing sun shine down on a mammoth lake where geese swim by in flocks. Peaches waddles away happily, and even Wilson jumps down from my pocket to give a sniff.

Most importantly, in the center of it all, on a large nest, sits the golden goose of our dreams. Jocelyn actually pinches me she's so excited, and so am I. She's real. The golden goose is real! She's not a myth! She looks just like a regular goose but is gold in coloring. Her feathers are so bright that they look like they're on fire. I greedily eye the golden eggs sitting around her. One of those eggs would set up my family for life if sold on the black market in Enchantasia.

"I've been expecting you," says the goose in a melodious voice.

"It talks!" Ollie exclaims. "This is goblin-tastic."

"Who? Me?" I ask, stepping closer.

The goose's beak moves to my right. "No, her."

"Me?" Kayla says in surprise.

"Your mother sent word," says the goose. "She told me of your journey, and I told her not to worry. With this set of companions, I knew you'd be well suited to complete your quest."

"Her mother is a *tree*," Jocelyn points out. "How would she send word?"

"Magical beings have a connection," says the goose. "We have a way of knowing when things are coming, both good and bad. This is how I know you've come to turn me over to him."

I feel guilty already. "I'm sorry." I pull the burlap sack we plan on carrying her in out of my uniform pocket. "We don't have a choice."

The goose doesn't move. "I will go without a fight, but I must insist that you do not touch the eggs I've already laid. A golden egg is sacred and belongs to this castle, even if I'm no longer in it. Understood?"

Her warning sounds ominous. "We understand." I should walk over and get the goose, but my feet won't budge. Maxine is already sniffling. Looking around the ancient shrine, I can't help feeling sad too. This goose has probably been here since before the beginning of time, and now we're going to give it to the person we despise the most. Who knows what he has planned for her? This feels so wrong, and yet it's the right thing to do, isn't it? "I'm sorry it has to be this way," I add. "If we don't bring you back, our lives will never be the same."

"And if you do bring me back, your lives will never be the same either," the goose says sadly. "I hope you realize doing someone else's bidding never ends well. The balance between good and evil is always a tricky one—and in your case, it's particularly murky—but I have no doubt that the man you want to give me to is evil. Sadly, when you give someone evil exactly what they want, they only crave more. This group wants all the power they can get their hands on."

"Did you say *group*?" I ask. "You mean Rumpelstiltskin, right?"

The goose almost looks like it's smiling. "You don't think he's the only one that wants me, do you? His master plan always involves more chess pieces than you're aware of." She appears to glance at Kayla.

"What if we just took one of your golden eggs instead?" Maxine suggests. "Maybe that would be enough to please him."

"One is never enough," says the goose. "Greed makes everyone want more. Once he has me, what will he want next, and what will he do with all the gold he acquires? What does he need it for? These are questions that you don't want the answers to. If he gets hold of me, I fear there are dark days ahead for Enchantasia."

I glance at Jax. He looks worried. So does Ollie. Hayley looks pained.

Jocelyn nudges me. "This is not a game," she whispers. "We need that goose. Go get her."

I step forward hesitantly. The goose doesn't try to flee. When I finally reach her nest, I place the burlap sack by her webbed feet. I can't bear to place her inside the bag. She has to walk in on her own. "I'm sorry," I say again. I've never been more torn. "Ouch!" I turn around. Peaches is pecking at me like crazy. She starts to quack, and Maxine rushes in between us.

"I can't let you do this," she says shakily. "Peaches is right! This golden goose shouldn't be enslaved to Rumpelstiltskin because we can't think of a way to beat him on our own!"

"Don't you think I wish I knew another way?" I argue. "You can't out-trick a trickster. We have to give him what we want if we want our lives back."

"Then we're not as clever as we think we are," Maxine says. "We're former thieves! We must know another way." She looks at the others. "Stealing the golden goose makes us as awful as he is, and you all know it."

"Maxine, please move," I say.

She shakes her head. "No. I'll protect this goose for the rest of my life if I have to, but I'm not moving."

"Push her aside," Jocelyn says. Ollie hits her. "What? We need that goose."

I step back, then forward again. I'm doing a dance with myself. "I don't know what to do!" I shout to the ceiling that looks like the real sky. Then I look to the one person I know will have the answer. "Jax?"

He shakes his head. "This is tough, but if we know what we're doing is wrong, how can it be the right thing to do?"

Maxine's left eye starts to wind up and spin. "Gilly, you've been my friend for a while now. You always defend me. Now I'm defending you. You won't be able to live with yourself if you do this. You might think you've won at first, but in the end, we'll all lose and you know it."

The golden goose listens to our conversation calmly. She seems to accept her fate either way, which is impressive, because I'm not sure what I'm doing is right. It would be so easy to nab that goose, but I'm not sure it will still get me what I want—freedom and Anna.

"I think Maxine is right," I say with a deep sigh. I glance at Kayla, who looks just as upset as I am. "The easy way isn't always the right way. The golden goose needs to stay exactly where she is."

Maxine cheers so loudly at the same time Jocelyn protests that none of us notice Peaches waddle up to the nest and begin sniffing the golden eggs. I watch in horror as the duck swallows one of the golden goose's eggs whole!

"Peaches!" I cry. The goose told us her eggs were not to be touched. *Fiddlesticks. We're done for.*

"Peaches, what have you done?" Maxine scolds as the duck lets out a loud burp.

We all watch and wait for Peaches to start choking like she usually does before she coughs something back up as an entirely new object. But this time she gives a small hack, then rolls out a golden egg. Maxine picks it up.

"How is the egg still an egg?" Maxine asks. "Whenever Peaches eats something, it always comes back up as something else we seem to need more."

"Maybe what you need is a decoy," says the goose, and we watch as Peaches starts to honk madly and shake. "I can help with that."

"What's wrong with her?" Maxine cries as Peaches spins around. When she's done spinning, she's transformed into the most beautiful goose I've ever seen. Her feathers are as white as snow. Her beak as shiny and orange as a beak should be. Her eyes are small and black and look much kinder than Peaches's menacing ones. The duck sneezes, and her appearance waffles. For a split second, she looks like Peaches again.

"What just happened?" Maxine asks.

"Magic," explains the goose. "Eating a golden egg will transform you—for a little while at least."

Jax takes the egg from Maxine. "If that's true, Stiltskin may believe Peaches is the golden goose. Especially if we make him think Peaches laid this golden egg."

"Trick him at his own game," Kayla agrees. "That could work!"

As I stare at Peaches, I think of what Red said about her mock magic capes: sometimes you just have to believe something is real to make it true. Maybe I need to start believing in myself. I'm a smart girl. Maybe I *can* out-trick Rumpelstiltskin. If I can do that, who knows what else I'm capable of?

"I think you're right," I add. "If we have the egg, and Peaches's magic holds, we might be able to convince Stiltskin this is actually the golden goose."

"But what if he can see us and he knows what we're up to?" Hayley asks worriedly.

"Child, he can't see in here," the goose says. "He may have seen your quest, but what happens in this castle is only mine to view. Since you are honoring the sacredness of this place, I will honor your quest and offer you this golden egg as a reward to do with as you please."

"He doesn't know if the goose is really golden colored, does he?" Ollie asks.

"Even if he does, we can fix that," Jocelyn says. She waves her hand over Peaches, and the duck's feathers turn as golden as the golden goose's.

"I think this could work," I say excitedly.

"I hope it will for all our sakes," the goose says. "In return for allowing me to remain here, I will see to it that your path home is a quick and uneventful one. And, Kayla? My regards to your mother. I have a feeling you will be seeing her very soon."

Kayla's eyes well with tears. "Thank you. I hope so."

Jax smiles at me. "Let's go home and take back our school."

CHAPTER 20

Tricky Business

It takes a day's time, but before we know it, Red has led us to the edge of school grounds. "This is as far as I can take you," she says.

Fairy Tale Reform School stands tall in the near distance. I can tell something is different about the place the minute I lay eyes on the school. It's not just that the protective bubble shield is down—maybe to let us back in?—but there is a new black wrought-iron gate that wasn't there when we left, and the grounds are eerily quiet for the middle of the day. The students are not out playing, and the Pegasus stables look locked up tight. It's like the school has been abandoned.

"Where are you headed, Red? Back in there?" Ollie nods to the Hollow Woods.

Red pushes her long hair away from her face and smiles. "Yes. I like those woods a lot more than the village. Taking orders at the shop, being crammed in a tiny house rather than having a whole forest for my home—it's suffocating."

"But people love Red's Ready for Anything shop," Kayla says. "You are going to reopen, right?"

"Of course," Red says. "I know the village needs that shop now more than ever. Shoppers want to buy into the legend of Little Red Riding Hood because it makes them feel safer, even if at the end of the day, I'm just a girl who fought off a wolf. Just like you all fought off a bandersnatch. But we're all more than just our conquests, aren't we? Neither thing can define you if you don't let it."

Maybe I don't have to follow in Father's footsteps if I don't want to.

The only question is: What do I want?

The air on my face, the thrill and fear of adventure, the feeling I get when I pull off an impossible feat—those are the feelings I crave. I just have to figure out what path will give me those things. "Thanks," I tell Red. "I needed someone to say that."

She looks at me. "The only person you have to be true to is yourself." She glances at the bow and arrow on my shoulder. "You can keep that."

"I couldn't," I say. "You need a spare."

"I'll make a new one," Red says. "I think this one suits you, and it might come in handy at some point. You surprised me out there." She looks at each of us. "You all did." A wolf howls in the distance, and Red slings her bow over her arm. "That's my cue. Send Wolfington my regards."

"We will," I say, "and thank you. For everything."

Red pulls her brown hood over her head and looks at the goose riding in Jax's pack (we didn't want Stiltskin to see Maxine with Peaches). "Good luck in there. I hope the golden goose gets you what you want." With a nod, we watch Red retreat into the shadows. I keep my eye on her 'til she blends into the forest.

We're alone again. I hike the quiver higher on my back and hear the arrows clink. The feel of the bow in my hand gives me a certain calm.

"Let's go give Stiltskin his prize," I say, walking toward the gates.

I think about blowing the lock off with an arrow. It

would look cool, but my aim is still lousy. I'm relieved when the gate opens magically on its own.

"Uh-oh." Maxine nods to Peaches. The duck is oblivious to the fact her disguise is fading. For a split second, she looks like her ugly duckling self. Then her goose disguise takes over again. A single golden feather falls to the ground and turns white.

Kayla swoops it up. "I'll hold on to that."

"We still haven't figured out how we're going to get Peaches back after we hand her over," Maxine says anxiously as we cross the moat. "We can't leave her with him."

"We'll think of something," Hayley promises.

Hansel and Gretel are waiting at the front doors. They've got on special gold RS uniforms.

"What do you rejects want?" Hansel asks.

Jax turns around, revealing the pack on his back and Peaches, who thankfully does not quack and give herself away. "To give Mr. Stiltskin what he requested."

"Unless you think we should leave and keep his precious golden goose for ourselves," I add.

Hansel and Gretel look at each other in surprise. They whisper to each other, and Gretel takes off down the hall.

"Follow me," Hansel says.

He brings us straight to Stiltskin's office and closes the doors behind us. The headmaster is seated on his desk talking quietly with Gretel and a few other RS members. With a pang, I see Anna among the group.

Rumpelstiltskin stands on the desk when he sees us. "Well? Is it true? Do you have it? Hand it over."

The doors behind us burst open, and Blackbeard, Wolfington, and Harlow come racing in. Harlow has brought along Madame Cleo on her mirror.

"Ye best be standing down, Captain!" Blackbeard says. "Thar be no treaties without us teachers present."

"Someone has to make sure these children get a fair deal after the hogwash you made them sign." Harlow puts a hand on Jocelyn. "You're all alive and in one piece."

"You sound surprised," Jocelyn says.

Harlow purses her lips and looks darkly at me. "It was an impossible task and a deal I never would have made myself."

"Speaking of the deal, here's our end of it." I pull the pack off Jax's back with Peaches tucked inside. *Just hang on for a few more minutes, Peaches*, I beg. I place the bag on Stiltskin's desk, and Peaches walks out of it.

"Can it be?" Stiltskin slowly circles the duck, then reaches down and plucks a feather. Maxine gasps as Stiltskin holds it up to the light. He slowly smiles. "It's gold! It's really gold!"

"You have your golden goose," Wolfington says. "Now pay up."

"We'll make this easy and bring Flora to you," Harlow adds. Purple smoke fills the room. When it clears, Flora's statue is standing in the middle of his office.

"Now hold up your end of the deal," I say.

"Not until I see if this goose really does what it's supposed to." Stiltskin rubs his hands together. "Goose, give me an egg!" Kayla and I look at each other worriedly. I start to sweat as Peaches just looks at him. Stiltskin stomps his feet. "Egg! I want one! Now!"

Suddenly Jax and Ollie start to laugh. What are they doing?

"Don't laugh at the headmaster," Hansel barks.

"I'd think a man who wanted the rarest animal in the kingdom would know how she works," Jax says. "She can't lay an egg on command. She only lays one a week."

Clever.

"And you know that how?" Stiltskin asks.

Jax looks surprised. "It was on the scroll, sir, that is engraved on the wall in the castle we stole the goose from."

"Barely made it out of there alive," Jocelyn adds.

"We had to risk certain death several times," Ollie agrees.

"We fought a wild sea serpent and a bandersnatch," Hayley tells him.

"Bandersnatch?" Harlow asks. "There is no such thing."

"Tell that to the one we fought," I say.

Stiltskin scratches his chin and smirks. "No egg, no deal."

My heart is pounding as Maxine presents the last piece of our ruse.

"Well, we do have one." Maxine pulls the large golden egg out of her bag, and Stiltskin practically falls off his desk. His grayish tongue hangs out of his mouth as he reaches greedily for the egg. The RS squad leans in to get a closer look. "The golden goose laid this egg on our journey back to school."

He snatches it from her without a thank-you and rolls the heavy egg in his hands. He rubs it, bangs it on the table, and holds it up to the jar of magic beans I almost forgot about. "We have it! The gold is ours! All ours!" Stiltskin laughs crazily.

Maybe we've gotten in over our heads.

Wolfington clears his throat, and I look at him. He motions to the desk where Peaches is beginning to transform again. Thankfully everyone is so busy looking at the egg that they don't notice. We're running out of time.

"So we have a deal?" I press.

Stiltskin looks at me, then at the goose and the egg again. His smile is devilish in the low office light. "Deal." Our contract appears in his hands, and he tears it in two.

"Yes!" Ollie can't help but cheer.

I breathe a sigh of relief as Stiltskin pulls his wand out of his pocket and points it at the window. In the distance, I can see the trees that hold Kayla's family glow, then shimmer. As the trees fade away, three figures appear on the ground.

"Mother!" Kayla cries and looks at us with tears in her eyes. "I have to go to them."

"Go, child!" Madame Cleo tells her, and Kayla flies out of the office.

"Now Flora," Harlow insists, and Stiltskin waves his wand. The statue shimmers, then glows red, then silver before melting and revealing the Wicked Stepmother.

"*...not take them!*" Flora says, coming out of the statue

in mid-fight with Stiltskin. Her hand falls, and she looks at us in bewilderment. "What is going on?" She looks around. "Where am I? Is this my old office? What did you do to my office?"

"Speaking of, I believe part of the deal was that you leave Fairy Tale Reform School *and* break your contract with Flora," Harlow reminds him.

Stiltskin looks hungrily at the egg again and motions to Hansel and Anna to grab Peaches. As Anna scoops the duck up in her arms, I see Maxine begin to panic. I try to reassure her with my eyes that it will be okay. Anna watches us curiously.

"I want to get out of here before they arrive to try to steal the goose," he says.

They? That must be the *they* the goose was referring to.

Stiltskin waves his wand again, and a new contract appears. He holds it up to the light. "Our contract is null and void too." My friends and I can't help but cheer.

Harlow opens the door. "I believe you were leaving. Take your muffins with you."

"Aye!" Blackbeard says. "They don't agree with me." He lets out a foul burp.

Stiltskin waves the scent away. "Alas, that means your protection of this school is gone as well." I hear a rumbling and a pop from somewhere outside the walls. "Pity. You need protection now more than ever."

"What are you talking about, you little troll?" Harlow snaps.

Stiltskin gives a high-pitched laugh. "Wouldn't you like to know? Stiltskin Squad, let's leave while it's still safe."

Anna follows the others to the door.

I try to block her exit. My heart is beating out of my chest. "Please don't go," I say hoarsely.

Anna gently pushes me aside. "I'm going, Gilly, and nothing you say will change my mind. Please don't make a scene."

I want to make her see she's making a mistake, but I know I can't. Wolfington was right. Anna has to find her own way. "Please be careful," I say.

"Gilly," Maxine whispers.

Anna smiles ever so slightly and clutches Peaches tightly. "I will. Good-bye, Gilly."

"Anna, we must leave," Stiltskin says. "Wait. What is happening to my goose?"

Peaches is convulsing in Anna's arms. Her shakes are so

violent Anna's forced to put the duck down. I watch in horror as the goose's disguise starts to fade in front of Stiltskin.

"*No!*" Stiltskin jumps off his desk and races toward the goose, just in time to see it turn back in to an ugly duckling. Maxine rushes in and picks Peaches up. "*No! No! No!*" Stiltskin stomps up and down like my little brothers Han and Hamish do when they're mad. His face is wrinkled like a prune and bright red. He glares at me. "You tricked me! You tricked Rumpelstiltskin!"

"Yes, they did, and you can do nothing about it," Flora says, finding her voice again. "Be gone. You're no longer welcome here!" Wolfington looks menacing, even in human form. Harlow forms a purple fireball, and Blackbeard brandishes his sword. Madame Cleo's hair is a fiery red on the small mirror. We stand with our teachers.

Our message is clear: you can't mess with Fairy Tale Reform School.

Stiltskin lets out a scream of anger so loud that he looks like he might explode. He grabs the magic beans on his fireplace mantel before Jax can reach them. Rumpelstiltskin waves his wand at the fireplace. The stone pot inside it comes flying out, and Jax, Ollie, and I duck as it flies toward

Stiltskin. I watch as the pot morphs into a giant cooking pan with a handle as long as a flying carpet. He jumps on, and the others in his squad follow. Hansel and Gretel climb on and hold their hands out to Anna.

Anna looks from me to Stiltskin. Even seeing what she's just seen, her choice is clear. She doesn't reach for me. She reaches for Gretel. They pull her onto the cookware.

"I'll get you for this!" Stiltskin shouts. "You haven't seen the last of Rumpelstiltskin!"

With a final scream of anger, Stiltskin, his squad, and the pan zoom out of the room. We race into the hallway and watch them fly down the hall and burst out the castle doors.

Anna is gone, and I'm not sure she'll ever be back.

Happily Ever After Scrolls

Brought to you by FairyWeb—

Enchantasia's Number-One News Source!

Rumpelstiltskin Kicked Out of Fairy Tale Reform School!

by Coco Collette

In a remarkable twist of events, *Happily Ever After Scrolls* has learned that Rumpelstiltskin has been banished from Fairy Tale Reform School after he was tricked into breaking the deal that gave him control of the school in the first place.

"I am pleased to announce Headmistress Flora is once again in control of the school she founded, and Rumpelstiltskin is on the run," said Princess Ella in a statement she made with her former wicked stepmother and stepsisters by her side.

"I thought giving Mr. Stiltskin the reins to FTRS was a way to give FTRS greater protection, but I was wrong," Flora said. "I should have discussed it with the royal court and my staff, who would have told me I was making a grave mistake. Thankfully, justice has prevailed and Fairy Tale Reform School is safe once more."

"We're so thankful to have our mother back!" said

Azalea and Dahlia. "And we're thankful to the Fairy Tale Reform School students who risked their lives to help get her job back."

While Flora refused to comment on details, sources say a band of students led by Prince Jaxon; the Evil Queen's sister, Jocelyn; and Gillian Cobbler, the shoemaker's daughter, set off to complete a quest that would end Rumpelstiltskin's reign. They apparently succeeded.

"All students who were sentenced to Fairy Tale Reform School on their first or second offense under Rumpelstiltskin will be released immediately," said school spokesmirror Miri. "However, those who wish to stay and work on their transformations from wicked to good are more than welcome."

The Dwarf Police Squad and Chief Pete have their work cut out for them. Not only will they be hunting down Rumpelstiltskin for his illegal dealings with FTRS, but they will also be searching for the students who chose to follow Mr. Stiltskin. "His Stiltskin Squad is very loyal to him," explained Pete. "We're determined to help these students see the error of their ways and to bring them back home." One of those students is Gillian's younger sister Anna.

Newly reinstated Headmistress Flora is personally

overseeing those efforts. "I believe in our school mission wholeheartedly and want to see every citizen of Enchantasia reach their full potential—including Rumpelstiltskin. If I can be reformed, anyone can. I won't stop until goodness reigns in our kingdom. And I won't sleep 'til every Fairy Tale Reform School student is back under my watch or at home with their families."

In related news, the Dwarf Police Squad is urging villagers not to panic over a crop of beanstalks that appeared in the countryside and also on the grounds of Fairy Tale Reform School right after Rumpelstiltskin's disappearance. The DPS insists that rumors suggesting the stalks grew from magic beans are completely unfounded, but they have promised to investigate further. Enchantasia old-timers need no reminder of the great giant invasion that almost destroyed the kingdom and the magic beans that gave the giants entry. When asked for comment, Pete laughed. "There are no magic beans in Enchantasia. Villagers need to stop worrying!"

Check back soon on the hunt for Rumpelstiltskin!

Chapter 21

Heartbreak and Happiness

There is a light knock on my dorm room door, and someone tries to open it. A difficult task since I barricaded it shut.

"Go away," I mumble, pulling my covers over my head. Wilson squeaks in protest. He's been lying next to me on my pillow since I collapsed here a few hours ago. After Anna left Enchantasia with Rumpelstiltskin.

"Gilly?" Maxine's voice is softer than usual. I don't answer. "My key doesn't seem to be working. Open up. We just want to talk to you."

"There's nothing left to say," I yell. "Anna chose Stiltskin over me. End of story."

There is whispering, then someone fiddles with the

lock. I hear a click and the door opens. *Fiddlesticks.* I should have known thieves would know how to get through my barricade.

"That's *not* the end of the story." Ollie walks in with the others. "It's just the beginning of a new one. Look at all we did today—Flora's back in charge, and Kayla's got her family again. You should be proud of yourself. We beat Stiltskin at his own game."

"But I lost Anna," I say, getting choked up. I hide my face in the pillow.

"*Quack!*" Peaches rips my blanket off me and drags it away before I can stop her. Why, that little ugly duckling! I sit up and see Jocelyn, Maxine, Jax, and Ollie standing over my bed. Even Jocelyn looks somewhat concerned, which makes me start to cry.

Jax sits down and puts his arm around me. "There's nothing you could have done, thief. She made a choice."

"It was the wrong one," I say, sobbing. "I know I had to let her figure things out on her own, but what am I going to tell Mother and Father?"

"You know better than anyone, Cobbler, that everyone has to think for themselves," Jocelyn says. "The little fool will realize her mistake eventually and come crying back to your hovel of a boot."

I wipe my eyes and look up, pushing the purple strands of hair out of my eyes. That might be the nicest thing Jocelyn has ever said to me. "You think so?" The others nod.

"And if she gets into trouble, we'll go after her," Jax says. "You're stuck with us."

Peaches quacks. "And you too, Peaches," Maxine coos. "The other fairy pets will definitely treat you better after this quest, which means you can go back to sleeping in the classroom." Peaches quacks wildly. "Of course, you can stay here with Gilly and me, if that's what you want." Wilson stands up and squeaks. "You can stay too, Wilson."

"Great, our dorm room is becoming a zoo," I grumble.

The door to my room flies open again. "Sorry to interrupt." Hayley is out of breath. "I was packing to leave, but Miri beamed in and told me Flora needs to see us right away."

Anna has come back. I rush out of the room with the others behind me. We're back at the scene of the crime in minutes. We burst through the office door, and I'm momentarily confused as to where I am. Stiltskin's decor is gone, and Flora's is back as if she never left.

Anna is not there.

Instead, I find my other teachers huddled around Flora's desk examining some books and scrolls Stiltskin left behind. Even more surprising, Princess Ella and Rapunzel are with them.

Harlow looks up and scowls. "Well, don't just hover. If you're here to help, get over here and help us figure out what Rumpelstiltskin was doing at Fairy Tale Reform School."

Flora comes forward. "If you don't mind, I'd like to speak to them first, Harlow."

She looks pretty good for someone who was just encased in stone. Her black-and-white hair is perfectly styled in a classic bun. Her understated, monotone, tailored dress doesn't show a single wrinkle, and one of her favorite brooches is pinned to her collared dress shirt.

"Wolfington filled me in on your quest," she says. "I know I asked you all to stay out of this, but I owe you debt of gratitude. If you hadn't interfered, we may never have gotten rid of that trickster." She looks at me. "I don't want you to worry either. The royal court is already readying troops to go after the students that went with him. We'll have your sister back in no time."

I smile sadly. "She went willingly, like I'm sure many of them did," I say, and Flora looks surprised. "I guess they're looking for something FTRS can't give them."

"You're working with the royals on this mission?" Jocelyn asks with obvious disdain. Jax gives her a look. "Former villains and princesses working together is not natural."

Flora smiles. "No, it's not, but it is progress. If we all want to be better versions of ourselves, we have to learn to trust one another. I know my stepdaughter is an asset in helping us figure out why Stiltskin was after those golden eggs and what he plans on doing with them."

"I still don't like it," Jocelyn says.

"Let me show you something." Flora leads us down the hall to a circular atrium that keeps appearing and disappearing as we walk up to it. The trick is nothing new, but the statue standing in the middle of the space is.

"What is she doing up here?" I ask.

Alva's statue now sits in the middle of an atrium students use to make their way to class. The evil fairy's stone sneer is creepy, and students walking by pass quickly.

"I asked Professor Harlow to move her where everyone could see her," Flora says, touching the cold stone arm of her enemy. "Alva is the perfect reminder of what can happen when you put your own needs first. I almost let my fear destroy me and this school." She looks at us. "Taking up Rumpelstiltskin's offer to protect us was a gateway to evil. I knew better than to trust the likes of him, but I did it anyway because I was desperate and selfish—two things your *Sinister to Sweet* textbook tells us are never good to indulge in." We all nod.

"Headmistress Flora?" says a goblin girl with a box of belongings in her arms. Her parents are with her. "I just wanted to say good-bye and thanks for letting me go home." She eyes the Alva statue warily. "I, uh, hope I don't ever have to come back."

Flora laughs. "Good girl." She pulls a glowing blue card from her pocket and hands it to the girl's parents. "But if you ever need us, my door is always open." Flora looks at us. "I guess we need to sign pardons for the lot of you again too. Hayley already signed hers."

"You're leaving us?" Maxine asks.

"My heart belongs with the sea and my family. I need to go back," Hayley says and looks at Flora. "But the headmistress said I could visit. I'll see you all again." We all take turns hugging the mer-girl who helped save our skins and watch as she walks away.

"We're accepting visitors now?" Ollie asks.

"Yes," Flora says. "Visitation day is back, and so are the Pegasus Posts. Everything is as it was before. So if you will pop back to my office, I can get your paperwork so you can be discharged by nightfall."

I glance at Jax, Ollie, and Maxine. Jocelyn is unfazed—she isn't going anywhere—but I have a feeling the others are thinking the same thing I am: We don't want to go home to our old lives. We like our new ones.

"Actually, I wanted to talk to you about that," I say. Wolfington walks out to listen to our conversation. "I think I speak for all of us—you know, except Hayley—when I say we don't want to be pardoned."

Ollie raises his fist in the air. "Aye!" Jax and Maxine nod.

Flora looks baffled. "I don't understand. You've all transformed beautifully."

"In some ways, maybe, but we still have a lot of growing up to do," I say, and I see Wolfington's face break into a wolfish grin. "Most of us are only twelve. We have a lot of years to still screw things up and be bad again."

"Why would you want to stay here in the meantime?" Flora asks incredulously. "This is a reform school."

"Because we're still reforming," I say. "Before I came here, I thought the only thing I could be was a shoemaker, but everything you taught me has made me see that I don't have to be one just because my parents are. I can be whatever I want to be—even if I don't know what that is yet," I add hastily. "But what I do know is that all of us are more than just heroes. More than thieves or villains. We're a lot of things."

"The classes here can help us figure out what we want to do next," Jax adds.

Flora looks uncomfortable. "I'm sorry, but that is not how Fairy Tale Reform School was meant to work."

"Why not?" Ollie asks. "You run it. Why can't the school be whatever you say it is?"

"You told the students who were charged under Stiltskin that they could stay if they wanted," Maxine reminds her. "Why can't we?"

"Instead of kicking us to the curb when we start acting good, why can't you have a program for students like us who are still trying to figure things out?" Maxine asks.

Flora and Wolfington exchange glances.

Wolfington smiles at me. "It sounds like our mutual friend was a good influence on everyone in the Hollow Woods."

"She was. Now we don't want to just learn to be good," I explain. "We want to learn what we're good *at*."

"This might not be such a bad idea," Wolfington says. "We're all capable of taking on additional classes to teach. I know Harlow would love to be done with macting. She'd be game for some of these, and so would I. Continuing to grow and change is good for all of us."

"Perhaps you're right." Flora looks at us. "Okay, you may stay."

Our shouting and cheering echoes in the atrium.

Maxine tackles me.

"I'm so glad we're all staying together," she says, giving me a fierce hug.

"Me too," I say happily. For some reason, I find myself staring over her shoulder at the statue of Alva behind us. I know it's silly, but I have an uneasy feeling that I'm being watched. Alva's a statue, and yet…I stiffen.

"What?" Maxine asks, feeling me pull away.

I blink rapidly and stare at Alva again. Her sneer seems reserved just for me.

"I…no…I've got to be wrong," I say shakily. "I'm sure my mind is just playing tricks on me. It's been a long day."

"What?" Maxine presses again.

I feel cold all of a sudden too. My voice is barely more than a whisper. "I could swear I just saw Alva's fingers move."

"What?" Maxine says in a high-pitched voice. Her eyeball begins spinning wildly as we both step slowly toward the statue. We continue to stare at it, but nothing happens. We both laugh nervously.

"For the love of Grimm, we are losing it!" Maxine says and claps me on the back. I practically fall forward from the force and hit Kayla as she flutters down the hall at warp speed.

"Headmistress Flora! We need to talk to you!" Kayla's got other fairies with her, and I realize one must be her mother. They all have the same face and tiny pointy ears.

"No flying in the halls!" Miri scolds, appearing in an atrium mirror.

"No demerits for her today, Miri," Flora says. "The child has just been reunited with her family! Kayla, won't you introduce us before you continue shouting?"

Kayla lands on the ground and looks at us sheepishly. "Sorry. This is my mother, Angelina, and my sisters, Emma

Rose and Brooke Lynn." Two girls, a few years older than Kayla, stand on either side of their mother. All three curtsy. One girl has yellow hair like Kayla's, and the other's is red like her mother's. All four of them have the same amber-colored eyes.

Kayla's mother takes Flora's hands. "Thank you for taking such good care of my daughter in my absence."

Jocelyn coughs. "She lived with me and my sister, but whatever."

"I want to hear everything there is to know about my daughter and the work she is doing here, but unfortunately, now is not the time," the fairy says and looks at us. "The kingdom of Enchantasia is in great danger."

"So it's true?" Jax asks. "Those beans Stiltskin had were the real deal?"

"I'm afraid so," Kayla's mom says. "The leviathans are coming."

"The leviathans?" I ask.

Kayla's mother looks at me. "The giants from the clouds. Rumpelstiltskin has already planted the first seeds. There's no stopping their invasion now."

I hear Wolfington, Flora, and Jocelyn audibly inhale, and even I'm concerned.

Ollie's eyes bulge out of his head. "Jack and the Beanstalk giants?" He shudders. "I thought those beans were done away with."

"Jack has been a bad boy," Kayla's mom says. "I have seen him harvesting more in my dreams. We must prepare."

"Well, that boy is getting a sentence right away!" Flora prickles.

"Are you certain about this?" Wolfington asks Kayla's mother.

Angelina nods. "The first plants have been spotted in the countryside and on Fairy Tale Reform School grounds."

"Great! Another villain to deal with." Jocelyn groans. "And this lot is way bigger—literally—than any we've dealt with before."

"We can stop them," I say.

"It won't be easy—not with Rumpelstiltskin helping them," Jax says.

My friends and I look at one another. Another battle is brewing—one with the trickster who has my sister on his side and another with a race of giants the likes of which we've never seen in Enchantasia.

We won't stop 'til we get rid of them both.

Ollie grins mischievously. "So where do we start?"

We all smile, then sit down in the corridor and get right to work figuring out a plan. I look at my friends and smile. I'm home.

This is my life at Fairy Tale Reform School. Exciting, busy, and adventurous.

Exactly the way I want it to be.

Acknowledgments

Kate Prosswimmer—who took the Fairy Tale Reform School baton and ran with it. You have helped me flesh out this world in ways I never dreamed possible. Thank you for all your guidance—and your excellent story arc spreadsheets! To everyone at Sourcebooks, including Steve Geck, Margaret Coffee, Beth Oleniczak, Elizabeth Boyer, and the crackerjack team of Kathryn Lynch and Alex Yeadon, thank you for always making me feel like Fairy Tale Reform School is the only series you're working on (and I know it's so not!). You have helped this series soar. To Mike Heath, for creating such amazing covers that readers can't stop asking me about.

Dan Mandel, who has given the students at Fairy Tale

Reform School—and the whole kingdom of Enchantasia—a bright future I can't wait to share with readers.

Elizabeth Eulberg, the best sounding board ever. Kieran Scott, my cheerleader, Courtney Sheinmel for her generosity, and Jennifer E. Smith and Alecia Whitaker for their sound advice and friendship.

To the one and only Gilly Miller (and her mom, Marcy) for lending me her name. For Hayley Lennon, who was too young to remember being named in my first book—I hope you like your new animal-loving, mermaid self! For Lisa and AnnMarie Gagliano for having never missed a local book signing in twelve years! To my mom and dad, thank you for being perfectly okay with me not loving sports and instead encouraging my love of writing, reading (and dancing).

Always and forever, thank you to Awesome Aubrey Poole, who took a chance on Gilly and her band of merry semi-villainous kids. I will forever be grateful.

For Mike, for always making me feel like a princess, and to my prince charmings Tyler and Dylan who weigh in on all villains and beasties. I'm lucky to have such great champions and critics right in my own home! And to Captain Jack Sparrow, an excellent office mate and lap warmer.

And to the readers who have had so many incredible suggestions about which fairy tale characters they'd like to see drop into FTRS next, thank you for sharing your love of this world with your teachers and friends. Enjoy your time at Fairy Tale Reform School, but don't get in trouble for staying up too late reading!

About the Author

Jen Calonita is the author of the Secrets of My Hollywood Life series and other books like *Sleepaway Girls* and *I'm with the Band*, but Fairy Tale Reform School is her first middle-grade series. She rules Long Island, New York, with her husband, Mike; princes Tyler and Dylan; and their Chihuahua, Captain Jack Sparrow, but the only castle she'd ever want to live in is Cinderella's at Walt Disney World.